A SMALL
CHARRED FACE

KAZUKI SAKURABA

A SMALL CHARRED FACE

KAZUKI SAKURABA

TRANSLATED BY JOCELYNE ALLEN

HAIKA
SORU

SAN FRANCISCO

A Small Charred Face
HONTO NO HANA WO MISE NI KITA by Kazuki Sakuraba
Copyright © 2014 Kazuki Sakuraba
All rights reserved.
Originally published by Bungeishunju Ltd. in 2014.
English Translation © 2017 VIZ Media, LLC.

Cover Illustration by George Cotronis
Cover and interior design by Adam Grano

HAIKASORU
Published by VIZ Media, LLC
P.O. Box 77010
San Francisco, CA 94107

www.haikasoru.com

Library of Congress Cataloging-in-Publication Data

Names: Sakuraba, Kazuki, 1971- author.
Title: A small charred face / Kazuki Sakuraba ; translated by Jocelyne Allen.
Other titles: Hontào no hana o miseni kita. English
Description: San Francisco : Haikasoru, 2017.
Identifiers: LCCN 2017020679 | ISBN 9781421595412 (paperback)
Subjects: LCSH: Vampires–Fiction. | BISAC: FICTION / Romance / Gothic. |
    FICTION / Horror. | GSAFD: Horror fiction. | Gothic fiction.
Classification: LCC PL875.5.A39 H6613 2017 | DDC 895.63/6–dc23
LC record available at https://lccn.loc.gov/2017020679

Printed in the U.S.A.
First printing, September 2017

CONTENTS

1.
A SMALL CHARRED FACE

BAMBOO

The snow danced through the air. A dance of death. I alone was motionless, my fingers numb with cold. My hands, my feet.

My teeth began to chatter, pebbles clacking up against each other. If they had been flints, flames would have sprung to life in my mouth.

Was I going to die too?

+ + +

I could hear the warm blood flowing out of Mama's body from where she lay in the hallway, her long legs splayed. The slow oozing had been echoing in my ears like the trumpets of the apocalypse. My teeth were chattering in time with the music. My tears froze solid on my cheeks.

The glass doors leading out to the terrace had been left open; huge drifts of pure-white snow gusted in. The heavy velvet curtains flapped threateningly in the direction of the gilded Japanese-style floor desk under which I hid.

From the neighboring hall, I heard my older sister start to scream. I squeezed my eyes shut. My shaking started to take on a noticeable rhythm.

The men's feet on the hard floor reverberated throughout the house.

In between wailing sobs, my sister groaned, "Kill me, kill me."

"This is some house!" I heard one man say.

"Take a look at that! This fucking fancy piano," another commented. "The sofa. And these sculptures!"

"I can't take it. Kill—"

An irritated gunshot cut my sister off.

Instantly, my eyes flew open. The sky said evening. The blue-gray light of late winter, colored with despair, poured into the room. The snow grew heavier. I curled into a ball, clutched my knees, tried to make myself almost impossibly small.

I heard the echoes of rough footfalls.

"Said to kill everyone?"

"Yeah."

"We're done here then. The woman and the kids. Three servants. A cook, a cleaning woman, and a washerwoman. Five people."

"There's still the son. He's like ten or something. I've seen him before. No one's come across him, huh?"

"He's probably out somewhere. We'll wait downstairs. One shot through the door when he comes back and we're done."

"Ten, huh? If he's as cute as his mother and sister…"

"*Pft!* You do what you want."

The men's footfalls faded down the stairs. The curtains fluttered up again in the wind, a gust mixed with icy snow, the breath of the god of death.

They were getting drunk downstairs. The bodies of the servants were still there in the kitchen.

On the other side of the window, dusk was falling too slowly, taunting me. It felt like a hundred years had passed already.

This town was nothing but organization men and people under their thumbs. Even if I did manage to somehow make it out of the house, there was nowhere for me to run. Nowhere in the world. This was the end.

Night finally fell, painting the other side of the window a chilly ultramarine. Shivering, I crawled out from under the low writing desk. An unflinching farewell.

Sister.

The thought of trying to walk without making any noise set me to trembling so badly I couldn't stay on my feet. Crawling awkwardly on all fours, I went out into the hallway and slipped slowly past Mama into the hall beyond her. My sister's eyes were wide open and glassy; she was dead. Her hands were clenched into tight fists, and she wasn't wearing any clothes. Her prestigious junior high uniform, the dream of every girl, was currently spread out all over the room, strewn across the furniture.

I crawled over to her. With a shaking hand, I closed her eyelids. I touched a finger to the hole between her eyebrows. Her eyelids were cold already, but the wound opening still held a faint warmth.

My sister…

I heard a sound and quickly looked over my shoulder. It couldn't have been the men coming back up here. They were talking about something downstairs.

I strained my ears. The glass doors? Had someone come in through the open doors in the next room?

The chattering of my teeth stopped. I listened with my whole body, with every suspicious, wary nerve ending.

The faintest of footsteps. Feet shuffling. Feet dragging? Who?

Whoever it was cut across the room, stumbled upon the desk I had only recently been hiding under, and then came out into the hallway.

I drew closer to the hallway and peered out quietly. There was someone in the shadows. The light of the winter moon carved out the silhouette of a young man—not too tall, with broad shoulders. In the time it took me to blink, he crouched down soundlessly. Right where Mama had fallen.

I squinted harder into the darkness. Held my breath. And then…

Slp, slp, slp. I heard the sound of drinking. Blood.

In my mind's eye, I saw Mama half-naked, her gold blouse stained red, striped miniskirt ripped. The man pressed his mouth to her neck and slurped up her blood.

This…this wasn't someone from the organization. The clothes he wore, the way he looked were just too different. I mean, he wasn't even human.

I remembered a scary story my second papa had told me a long, long time ago about a race of monsters that came from deep in the mountains of China. They were called the Bamboo. And true to their name, they were monsters of those tall grasses, carnivorous plants that drank the lifeblood of humans and ate their still-living flesh. They were nearly human in appearance. But unable to stand under the light of the sun, they walked the night…

That's why you weren't supposed to go out walking alone after the sun set. The Bamboo would find you and eat you.

Mama had looked at me shaking in fear and laughed in her high-pitched voice. "Isn't that just a story to frighten children?"

And now Mama was dead, crumpled on the floor like a marionette with its strings cut, and something was eagerly lapping at her blood.

I heard a noise like a blade slicing through flesh. It was that...*thing* lifting his face. My whole body shook. My teeth started chattering like crazed castanets again.

The man seemed sincerely surprised to find a living creature before him. I couldn't see his face. Only the blood around his mouth was visible, glistening in the dark.

"You." Was he smiling? "You're seriously good at making yourself invisible, boyo!" Surprisingly, the voice fell somewhere between that of a boy and a young man. It was teasing and unexpectedly gentle.

"Who are you?"

"Bamboo."

"Do the Bamboo really exist?"

"What? You've heard of us?"

"You walk at night! Drink lifeblood! Eat flesh!"

"Dummy. We don't drink lifeblood. We have laws, y'know."

"Laws?"

The men downstairs stopped talking abruptly. The Bamboo held his index finger up to his lips. *Shh!* That finger also glistened with fresh blood.

I stared at him, bewitched. Strangely, I wasn't frightened, even though I had cried so hard when my second papa had told me the story. I mean, I was going to die either way.

Downstairs, the men started speaking again.

The Bamboo in front of me slowly began to move his

mouth once more, and something—hair wet with blood—bobbed up and down. "The smell of blood called out to me. I mean, this town constantly *reeks* of blood, y'know? All the different organizations fighting all the time. They never get sick of it. But what's the big hubbub here?"

"My papa slept with the boss's woman, and they found out," I replied, my voice absurdly calm. "He took the woman and the money and the goods and ran off. So they killed Mama and my sister and me tonight, as a lesson."

"Huh, makes sense. But you're still alive, aren't you?"

I closed my mouth.

There was a group of hitmen downstairs now, happily drinking the night away. Probably everyone in town knew by now that the only one they hadn't taken out yet was the son. I could never trust a living human being again.

But if I could choose the method of my death in a last moment of selfishness… Please, God. I took one step, then another, walking toward the unearthly monster.

"Huh? What?"

I reached out both hands. I wanted to be released from my terror! I'd had more than enough of this tired human instinct to survive working on overdrive, ordering me to run away, to push back against destiny, to fight desperately to live right up until the last, all despite the fact that the end result would be the same, no matter what I did—I would lose the battle and die. The finish line was the same. But somehow, I was supposed to fight, to resist. Any god that would order me to do something like that was a thoughtless, spoiled brat.

I heard muffled laughter—*heh heh heh*—and opened my eyes.

He was looking down on me, his own eyes large and turned downward at the corners, his eyelashes thick and long. In the darkness, his eyes and the red blood around his mouth alone seemed transparent; they shone with an eerie clarity.

"Meat on a plate then! Blood that flies into the cup! First time I've seen that!"

"Don't…make fun of me," I protested, my voice trembling. *Don't laugh at my last hope.*

The Bamboo stopped his snickering. And then he crouched down and met my eyes. "Hey, you're shaking." He touched my shoulders lightly, playfully exasperated.

"Okay, boyo," he said, kindly. "Listen up. We Bamboo have rules. Y'know? We have our own—well, I guess it's something like a government. It's different from the country you human beings have made, but it's ours. And we have our own strict laws. Or maybe you'd call them precepts? I dunno how it was in China in the beginning. I dunno anything about way back then. But for the Bamboo living in Japan right now, it's a thing that you're only allowed to eat the dead. Like, we can only drink the blood of the dead." The Bamboo cocked his head to one side slowly. "But maybe this is all over your head?"

"What happens if you break the rule?"

"You get locked up for sixty years! They stuff you in a barrel and bury you in the ground!"

"You'd be an old man after that!"

"Huh? Would not. Why would I?" the Bamboo retorted, curiously.

Now that he mentioned it, my second papa had said that

the Bamboo were young forever. They never aged. And he said that, just like bamboo, just once, when they're around 120 years old, they bloom, bursting into a spray of white flowers. Then they disappear into nothingness.

The one who had left this morning with the boss's woman and money and stuff was my fourth papa. He had come to Japan from somewhere in Latin America. He'd joined one of the organizations in this town, the one for people from the same place as him, and had moved up through the ranks. After my poor Japanese mama had latched on to him, life in our family had suddenly gotten a whole lot easier. But that had ended this morning.

The wind whirled and carved out a circle, winding through the room. In the blink of an eye, the Bamboo was sitting on the edge of the open window. He waved. "Later, kid!"

I cocked my head to one side and stared at him. The icy light of the moon illuminated his face for the first time. His large eyes were dry like desert sand. His eyebrows were thick, and a beard covered the lower half of his face. His clothing was oddly neat. It wasn't expensive like the stuff Papa and Mama wore, but it was well cut, and he wore it with dignity. With his sharply defined features, he looked half-Latino and half-Japanese. The way the moonlight caught his dark skin made me think, *Aah, if only he didn't have that beard, he could be one of those beautiful boys the girls love.*

But if the Bamboo had a rule, I guess that was that. I smiled. *Goodbye, Bamboo.* So the story about the bloodsucking grass monsters was true, after all. I wouldn't tell anyone, though, just because I'd seen one. I mean, I had no tomorrow.

Perhaps the men had heard our footsteps; there was

an intent silence coming from down below, like they were straining their ears, listening. This was followed by the sound of feet climbing the stairs. The rustling of guns being drawn.

The Bamboo twisted his face up.

The footsteps came closer.

My teeth chattered. My whole body shook again.

My sister's wide-open eyes. Her scattered uniform. Her trampled dignity. Would I also tell them I couldn't stand it and beg them to kill me? The warmth of the wound between her eyebrows. My sister. The footsteps reached the hallway. My terror made me a stone statue. I closed my eyes.

Do the weak not even get to choose the way we die? Preyed upon, tormented, we die.

"The rule's absolute," the Bamboo muttered, almost like he was making excuses. "I'd get more than the barrel underground for sixty years for this. I mean, punishment by fire's no joke, y'know? It's pretty much the most painful way for us to disappear from this world. So it's a no-go. Sorry, 'kay?" For some reason, the words that followed sounded like he was whispering right in my ear. "I don't owe you anything. Right? Yeah?"

What was he talking about?

The men approached from the hallway. They entered the room, moved to turn on the light and banish the pitch-black dark.

"Aah, dammit… Goddammit! Quit making that face at me!" The Bamboo clicked his tongue surprisingly loudly. "Quit crying!"

Click. The lights came on. I knew even with my eyes shut that they were painfully bright.

Aah, they've finally found me. It's the end of today, of tomor-row, of yesterday, of forever.

And then the wind was roaring in my ears.

♦ ♦ ♦

When I opened my eyes, I was flying through the night sky, the snow fluttering down like a lie, like a dream. It was beautiful.

Was I dead? It was surprisingly comfortable. I felt no pain, no shame. It felt somewhat anticlimactic.

I looked to one side. I was wrong. I wasn't dead. The Bamboo was clutching me for some reason; we flew through the air in a wobbly fashion that did not inspire confidence. The chill sky was painted ultramarine. The cold clung to everything. I slowly looked back over my shoulder.

The peninsula jutted out into the Pacific Ocean. *It looks just like Santa Claus's boot, eh?* my sister used to say, giggling. A little place in eastern Japan. Several narrow roads wound around the hill toward the ocean like capillaries. At the top was the domain of the very wealthy, where we lived. Mansions gave way to shacks and huts the closer you got to the ocean. There was basically no movement between the town at the top of the hill and the slum at the bottom. Almost like they were separate countries.

I had been convinced that I'd never get out of there alive. But the sumptuous estate, complete with pool, gradually receded from my sight, along with the luxurious town laid out like some kind of Shangri-la.

"So you saved me?" I asked the Bamboo's face in profile.

"Swear your loyalty to me."

"Let me think about that."

"You cheeky brat! And you're a crybaby on top of that!"

A warm relief spread through me, although the core of my heart was still frozen with terror. But, bit by bit, I was finding my way back. And then an abnormally powerful desire to sleep, like an evil spirit, assaulted my consciousness.

"Hey!" I said, rubbing my eyes.

"Quiet! I'll drop you, y'know. I'm trying to concentrate on flying here!"

"You have a name?"

"Course I do."

"I'm Kyo."

"Mustah."

"…Mustah!" Murmuring the name, I clung tightly to his solid chest. It was cold like a corpse's. The temperature of the night. The faint green scent of bamboo clung to him.

This is my Bamboo! I'll swear my loyalty. Not out loud, though.

I hugged him tightly.

My Bamboo was unfortunately not very good at flying, it seemed. If he were driving, he would have had one of those NEW DRIVER stickers on the bumper to warn others on the road. Or maybe it was because I was too heavy? Mustah swung dangerously back and forth, threatening to drop me into the abyss at any second as we floated awkwardly toward the bottom of the peninsula shaped like Santa Claus's boot, toward the impoverished town near the ocean.

Mustah.

Mustah.

◆ ◆ ◆

"Back when I was a human, okay? When I was small like this kid here, someone gave me this jar of jam. 'Cause I was poor, y'know? I held on to it like it was made of gold."

Ah, Mustah's voice. I heard it from far away.

"I lapped up a teeny bit of it every day. It was like, as long as I was careful like that, I could savor it forever. So basically—how about we put the kid on the shelf like that jam, and we just drink his blood bit by bit? Good idea, right? Just enough so he doesn't die."

"Mustah, you—he's tiny," someone else said. His voice was higher and thinner than Mustah's, but it was a man's. Whose?

"So then we go hard!"

"Honestly. Let's have this be the last of threatening children. It's just embarrassing, okay?"

"So then, like—hey! I'll eat you all up tonight, damned brat!" There was the sound of a door being yanked open.

I curled up more tightly into myself and rubbed my eyes.

"Oh, come on. He's sleeping." Mustah sounded disappointed.

"Humans sleep at night, Mustah. And there's no point in going out of your way to threaten him after you saved him, now is there? You crossed a dangerous bridge because you wanted to. You're a weird one."

"Excuuuuse me!"

"What?"

"You're in this now too, Yoji." His name was Yoji then? The other person with the quiet voice.

"Mm. Well, yeah."

"We're definitely going to have to leave him."

It was quiet for a while.

"He's really out, eh? Almost like a picture of an angel. Kids have such round faces, don't they? I-I just had no idea."

Someone's finger touched my cheek lightly. It was so cold that it startled me and made me shiver, and my eyelids twitched as if to open. But I was sinking down to the bottom of a deep sleep, and I didn't know what was what anymore.

"He's super warm. Like a fire!"

"Right?"

"Mustah… This boy's *alive!*" The thin voice shook with extreme emotion.

From farther away, I felt like I heard a dry laughter too. I didn't know whose voice it was. Maybe Mama's. No, maybe God's. As if to say, "See? You cursed and railed at me, but I saved you in the end, didn't I?" The darkness of night grew steadily thicker.

When I woke up, it was past noon. How deeply and how long had I slept?

I looked around and found I had been put to sleep on top of a pile of towels spread out over a wooden floor. The pile was neatly arranged, but for all that, it felt kind of strange to be directly on the floor.

I was in a living room, about sixteen and a half square meters, furnished with an old but well-maintained sofa and wooden table, along with an antique organ. I was cold; a shiver ran through me. One wall of the room was taken up entirely by glass doors, which had been left slightly open. I could see the pale sand of the beach and the ocean beyond it. Wind coming in off the sea surged inside and whirled around me, an invisible vortex. I hurriedly got to my feet and yanked the doors shut. My fingers and toes were nearly frozen.

I slumped down absently onto the sofa. And then I listened for the presence of anyone else. It appeared I was alone.

The room was small and modest, totally unlike the mansion I'd lived in until the day before. But it was clean and quiet. There were some *onigiri* rice balls, a pack of fried eggs, and a plastic bottle of juice on the table. I guess the Bamboo had bought them somewhere. My stomach growled abruptly, and I reached out to the table. I saw that my arm was pale, bloodless. But it had finally stopped shaking.

The cold onigiri was delicious. The fried eggs too. Because I was alive.

A change of clothes had also been left for me, so I spread them out, thinking maybe they'd protect me against the cold. A black winter skirt made out of heavy fabric, a white sweater, and a silk blouse with a square necktie. Girl clothes. I sighed in disappointment. Did I maybe look like a girl? No, that couldn't have been it. I mean, he'd kept calling me *boyo, boyo*.

Wondering curiously about how I'd ended up with girl clothes, I pulled the sweater on and then settled back down onto the sofa, curling myself up into a ball.

The old wall clock ticked out a quiet rhythm. When I sat there silent, visions of all the things I'd lost the night before began to shoot through my mind. My sister's screams, her uniform strewn about, Mama's long legs splayed, the snow blowing in through the window, the black shadow of a man drinking blood…

I leaped to my feet. After carefully inspecting the entire room, I slid the glass door open and stepped resolutely outside.

The ocean was calm, the chilly waves glittering. Gray sand blown up by the wind covered the wooden deck, and the grains flickered and shone as they caught the light. The wooden bench set out there was also an antique and well cared for. I stepped down onto the beach before I realized my feet were bare. The sensation of cold sand on the soles of my feet was electric.

When I looked at the house from outside, I saw that it was a small bungalow. Squarish, made of wood. Perhaps the exterior had been damaged; it was reinforced here and there with plywood and sheet metal, which came together in some kind of mysterious pattern. I looked around to see similarly rough houses dotting the area. The town continued down the peninsula toward the ocean, over a hill of impoverished shacks, and finally reached the shore. This was apparently the end of it.

I went inside. It was cold.

I opened a door that led farther into the house and found a tiny kitchen on my left. It appeared to be mostly unused and more of a storage space piled high with cardboard boxes. An oversized commercial refrigerator rose up from among them, emitting an unpleasant electrical hum. On my right was a small room the light didn't reach.

I stepped inside. There was a large wooden chest situated imposingly on the floor there, seeming just as out of place as the refrigerator in the kitchen. I went over and kneeled down before it. Pressed my cheek to it. It was cold. I listened carefully, but I couldn't hear anything.

I tried calling him. "Mustah." My Bamboo. I suddenly felt very fond of him, and I called his name again. "Mustah!" I got no answer. But I had this feeling that he was there.

"Hey, Mustah?" My own voice was surprisingly sweet. I reached out a pale arm and slowly lifted the lid of the chest.

Instantly, I was assaulted by cold air. My breath froze into a white puff. This was the coldest place in the house, a deeper freeze than outside. I peeked in, terrified, and finally, from within the white fog, two faces appeared. Like waxwork, motionless. Two adult men facing each other, almost embracing, their eyes closed. They weren't wearing clothes; they were totally naked.

One had a strong face with dark skin. His long eyelashes created a shadow below his eyes. *Mustah*. The other one was Asian with tawny skin and fine features. His eyelids were chilled and seemed sad somehow, while his thin lips were pursed tightly in a way that made him seem high-strung. This in contrast to Mustah's sunny eyes and half-open mouth.

Their right fists touched their exposed chests. It was like they were dead. The words "lovers' suicide pact" floated up in my mind. A sweet, eternal rite of people in love.

And then my heart throbbed painfully. It felt bad. What was this emotion?

Right. The other voice I'd heard last night, that gentle, thin voice, had probably been his. The second I had this thought, Mustah's eyes snapped open, the dead coming back to life. I was surprised but not scared. I had no doubt used up my lifetime allotment of terror the previous night.

His black eyes alone moved, unnaturally, like those of a mechanical doll. His waxen body didn't so much as twitch. The skin of his face was also taunt, artificial.

"Wait. Until night. Little Kyo."

"…But it's cold."

"Ooh, cold?" There suddenly came a very displeased voice, and the cold air shuddered fiercely, pushing me back.

My hands slipped off the lid of the chest, and it fell back down with a thud.

✦ ✦ ✦

"Right! Humans get cold, y'know, Yoji! I totally forgot!"

"They do, huh? I didn't know that to begin with. So listen then."

"Huh? What?"

"You have to take proper care of this kid, okay, Mustah?"

"…Yeah."

"Don't make it seem like such a huge hassle. You're the one who brought him home. And."

"Hmm?"

"And look how happy you are now. Being reminded after all this time that human beings get cold."

"…Well, there is that."

The start of the night. The winter day had quickly drawn to a close, and the moon had begun to shine coldly when the lid of the chest clattered and opened up. The grass monsters were awake. Despite the fact that he had only just ordered Mustah to take care of me himself, the one called Yoji pulled a coat over his naked body, then hurried out to get me an antique heater. He turned it on, and warmth began to fill the room. I thanked him with a smile.

And then the first ritual of their day began. Still naked, they went around to light all the candles in the candlesticks scattered around the house. Like it was something very important. Very carefully, one by one. The room brightened faintly. Then they took turns washing their faces before turning toward each other and vigorously combing one another's hair. They slipped their arms through the sleeves of starched cotton shirts. Mustah's was black, Yoji's white. They fixed each other's collars, and then Mustah pulled on leather pants, while Yoji dressed in jeans. They inspected the other's appearance very carefully. Rather than any kind of intimate gesture, this dance looked more like the habit of long years.

Crouched in front of the heater, I felt a strange restlessness. "Hey? Why?"

"Huh?" Mustah looked back at me.

"Um, I was just wondering why you don't do all this yourself, but do it to each other instead. It's weird."

Mustah indicated the window with his chin. The glass of one wall, naked of curtains or any other kind of covering, hazily reflected the inside of the room. Sofa, table, organ. Wall clock. Heater. Me crouching. But the figures of Mustah and Yoji standing facing each other were nowhere to be seen.

I stood up in surprise. "Neither of you is there!"

"That's why." It was Yoji who answered. He looked down at me and smiled gently.

"So then." I wound myself around him. "You've never seen your own face in a mirror?"

"*I* have, a long time ago." Mustah shrugged lightly.

"Not once," Yoji replied softly.

Apparently finished dressing, Mustah bobbed his head around, satisfied. And then he reached a hand out to the bookshelf against the wall where an antique camera sat. "And we show up in media. So if you really *have* to see your face, you can just take a picture."

"Wow."

"Digital's no good, though. No one knows why. We show up in print photos. And films, y'know? Like, if you got an eight-millimeter motion picture camera, you could get us moving." Mustah lifted up an old black machine and laughed playfully. He turned the old camera toward me.

I looked up absently, and Yoji came over and pretended to bite my neck. But playing like this was apparently not in his nature, so, blushing, he stopped. Mustah handed him the camera and delightedly lifted me up with one hand. He tossed me at the ceiling and then caught me when I came back down. That hard lump, the chunk of ice in the bottom of my stomach, melted. Being alive was fun again. I squealed with laughter. The camera followed us.

Then Yoshi pulled something out of the large refrigerator. Red liquid in a plastic bag. They poured it into pottery that looked like a Japanese-style flower vase and set it down on the table. They poured from this into vessels like teacups, like large sake cups, before sitting down across from each other and drinking from them quietly.

From time to time, they talked, haltingly. Maybe because they'd been together for so long, their conversation was the brief back-and-forth of close friends; they understood each other with a few easy words. I settled into Mustah's lap. My heart made a curious snapping sound again.

They drank the blood slowly. Like they were enjoying fine sake. The meal of the Bamboo in Japan today…

I sat between the two of them and quietly compared their

faces. Mustah's was sullen, while Yoji's still sported a faint smile. Both of them were well-mannered, calm, and quiet. *Aah*, I thought. *Now I get it. The town at war I lived in until yesterday is a much bloodier place than this one.* I also thought that was strange somehow.

♦ ♦ ♦

"The mountains of China? Well, I guess that's basically it. To be honest, I don't really know either. What I heard is that we traditionally lived somewhere deep in the mountains in the middle of the continent. But people gradually came in and opened those areas up too. It got harder to hide. So sometime in the last century, one group just up and moved to Japan, y'know? Came out from the mountains, down the river, crossed the ocean."

"Mustah's from the other side of the ocean too."

"Am not! I'm a Japan-born Bamboo!"

I didn't really understand.

"We're all over the place."

"Well, not really. After that group came to Japan, they splintered into several smaller groups and scattered. I heard that there's not even a single one of us in some areas. There's such a mess of different tribes and people on this peninsula, so it's easy to live in hiding here, y'know? This might be the town with the most Bamboo in all of Japan. We have, like, meetings on nights of the full moon."

"Like cats!"

"Not cats. Bamboo."

"Right."

"About two hundred of us, maybe? Or wait, maybe more. I dunno. Never properly counted."

"Are you called Bamboo in China too?"

"Dunno. Although I think maybe we started being called that after we came to Japan. In China, they probably called us something Chinese."

"So how can we tell who's Bamboo and who's not?"

"No idea. Well, anyone who works the night shift and doesn't eat, they're definitely suspicious!" Mustah stood up nonchalantly, and I tumbled from his lap. I sat on the floor and looked at the two of them.

Mustah's body odor, the faintest scent of bamboo, remained in my nose. I liked this smell.

Yoji was walking through the room at a measured pace, cleaning almost neurotically and closing up the doors. Mustah just opened up the cupboards, picked up the camera, and touched his beard busily. His face in profile seemed quite whimsical. Finally, Yoji grabbed his endlessly dawdling partner by the arm and practically yanked him toward the front door.

I became uneasy. "Where are you going?"

"We work at night, like I said," Mustah said, sounding annoyed, his back to me, before he turned around abruptly. A grin made his beard shake.

"We're assistant nurses," Yoji told me, hands firmly clasped around Mustah's shoulders, dragging him along. "Emergency room. They're understaffed, so it's easy to get hired." And then he screwed up his face like a worried mother. "Please go to bed. Don't go walking around at night. It's not safe."

"Because the Bamboo are also walking around at night!" Mustah added, jokingly, and laughed at his own words.

I waved. The pair looked relieved, and each returned the gesture in his own way.

I heard something like a strong wind blowing. The thought had no sooner crossed my mind than they were gone. That was indeed the way a monster disappeared, like a whirlwind of the night.

I took over the sofa, covered myself in towels, lay down, and fell asleep, but only for a brief period. I opened my eyes in the middle of the night. I cleared my ears. There was no one there.

The candles in the room flickered restlessly in ancient candlesticks of Japanese, Western, Chinese, and Persian design. They had burned down a fair bit; the flames were low.

I suddenly thought of my sister. How she had been a good person. Kind. She had never asked too much of the help. She had treated Mama well too. And me. She had been shy only with men, and faced with one, she would turn red, unable to speak at all. Those wide-open eyes of hers came back to me.

There was something hard inside the sofa, and the corner of it jabbed my back. I reached my hand back, ready for anything.

It was a book with a red cover. An old collection of poems. When I opened it, I found traces of tears on the pages. Chinese poetry maybe. I tried to read the poems. But they were too difficult, and I simply couldn't see why they had made the owner of the book cry.

Finally, one candle and then another disappeared with a sizzle, until at last the room was pitch-black, and my body was tossed into a darkness like death.

✦ ✦ ✦

I awoke suddenly. I felt like I had heard the sound of wind.

I got up from the sofa, and a man in a white shirt sound-lessly appeared, moving with beautiful grace on the beach on the other side of the glass. I could see he hadn't come from either side but from above. Yoji. Remembering Mustah's dangerous, wobbly flight last night, I had the vague thought that Yoji was maybe the better flier.

And then a man in a black shirt plummeted down, off-balance, just barely managing not to tumble to the ground. My Bamboo! He smiled, almost self-consciously. Like he was saying, *I just can't fly too good.* My heart started pounding again.

Now Yoji flew, gliding along the surface of the earth, opened the window, and came into the room. He was uncharacteristically flustered, and once he'd stopped, he did another empty spin right there in midair.

Dawn was imminent. The morning was approaching across the surface of the ocean.

I could see that the faces of the two Bamboo were both paler than they had been at the start of the night. Maybe because morning was near. In one hand, Yoji held a liter-sized pack of blood. I assumed they had bought it at the hospital where they worked.

"Little Kyo, it seems you are a wanted man." For all his hurried flying, Yoji sounded cool and relaxed. I stared at him blankly.

"That boss guy you were talking about." Mustah walked, rather than flew, in. "Heard he's got a bunch of feelers out for a little boy they accidentally let get away in the town up there. I seriously doubt they'd come all the way down here, though. And the people who live here have basically nothing to do with them. But Yoji's all worried and kicking up a fuss, all 'Oh, the danger!'"

"Mustah, it's just like you said. We should make him wear a disguise. Even after he grows up too. Definitely."

After I grow up?

Mustah nodded. "Take a look, Kyo!" And he pointed at something.

The change of clothes that had been left on the table. The silk blouse and the long black skirt. The girl's school uniform?

I got up in a panic. "I won't. No way."

"Look, you. They've got their eyes peeled for a boy, right? So if you be a girl and stay here for a while, like, once you grow up, maybe..." Mustah cut himself off and met Yoji's eyes. They nodded at each other.

What was it?

I was upset, but the two grown-ups talked me down, and eventually I resigned myself to putting the uniform on. Yoji stared hard at me when I was naked, very interested somehow. "Quit it," I said, turning my back to him.

The blouse with the square necktie. The white sweater. The black skirt with the pleats. I stared fearfully at my reflection in the glass. I was still holding myself like a boy, so the effect was weird.

Yoji and Mustah both let out a sigh, like they could finally relax. They flopped down on the sofa on either side of me at the same time.

The only thing reflected in the glass was the new me; the two men seated behind me to my right and my left were nowhere to be found.

Mustah slapped my butt hard. "I don't know if you really look like a girl, though. But people here have too much on their own plates to go around looking at a kid in a skirt and spending brain power wondering if she isn't really a boy. Right, Yoji?"

Yoji was silent, looking at me with concern. And then said, "Yes."

Mustah let out another relieved sigh. The scent of bamboo wafted up to my nostrils.

They stood up and started to undress. This part, they each did themselves. Mustah let his clothes fall where he stood, and Yoji picked them up and folded them.

I got sleepy again and rubbed my eyes with the back of my hand.

Weak light came in through the glass, as if to announce that morning would soon arrive. So did that mean that human time was finally starting? The gentle grass monsters slipped sluggishly into the small, cold room at the back. They opened the lid of the chest, and a chill instantly filled the air. The lid slowly closed, and all sense of their presence disappeared.

I went to sleep again on the sofa. Wearing the girl clothes.

◆ ◆ ◆

That night, I had a dream. In it, I was still in the town above. I was desperately fleeing along a dark road at night. The men were chasing me. I ducked into an alley to catch my breath. When I looked back, the men weren't running along the road, but flying through the air, ready to dance down at any moment and snap my windpipe. *Ah! Bamboo are after me!* I started to scream.

Then another Bamboo flew in from somewhere... Mustah, maybe?

It *was* Mustah!

He flicked a hand out, wrapped his arm around my waist, and then immediately flew up high into the night sky. His flight was a little erratic, but he skillfully lost my pursuers, and we kept flying, drifting through the starry sky.

Thank goodness. You saved me...

Grinning, I started to say something in his ear. But even though it was a dream, my eyelids suddenly grew incredibly heavy. I started to drift off. Secure, I fell into a deep sleep in that beautiful starry night. The wind on my skin felt good too, and even as I slept, an unconscious smile crept across my face.

SCHOOL

Wake up in the morning. The antique alarm clock Yoji bought me rings at seven sharp. Wash my face, tie my hair—now down to my shoulders—back into pigtails. Get dressed.

Breakfast is always on the table. Onigiri rice balls, bread in packages. Sometimes several cans of fish are piled up there for some reason.

Yoji comes flying home at dawn with a pack of blood in one hand and food for me in the other. He leaves the food on the table with a note, but from time to time, Mustah plays games with me and hides the stuff inside a cupboard or something. One time, when I can't find it and have to leave with an empty stomach, Yoji gets mad at him, and Mustah is sad.

Black leather bag I carry on my back. Inside, a bundle of papers copied from the textbook and my notebooks. Run out of the house.

The Bamboo are asleep. Actually, you could even say dead maybe. They won't come back to life until nightfall, those mysterious grass monsters from the other side of the ocean.

◆ ◆ ◆

"Morning, Nako!"

In a corner of the prefab school lot, the morning was dazzling with the light bouncing back off the ocean. Beads of sweat dripped down my face.

The lower town no longer had a respectable school. There was just a small cram-school-type place, like the temple elementary schools they used to have way back when. Prefab buildings on the verge of crumbling dotted the empty factory lot, one unit for each grade. And a teacher in each one too. I went to this school dressed as a girl, under the name of my dead sister. A disguise so the men from above wouldn't find me.

I was an excellent student. Because the only thing I could do to stay alive right then was study. If I was going to stay in this town forever, I would need something. Maybe I could be a teacher. Being an assistant nurse like Mustah and Yoji wouldn't be too bad, either, but I'd probably be stuck in a hand-to-mouth life with a job like that.

…If I was going to live. And so I worked.

The boy who called out to me had become a friend. He had dark skin and long eyelashes. He was super skinny but always full of energy. He wasn't good at school, so I'd help him sometimes. I was easy to talk to for a girl. He often said to me, "Nako, you just really get stuff." Of course. I was really a boy, after all.

"Niita! Morning!"

"Lemme see your homework."

"Yeah, yeah."

We went into the classroom, pushing and shoving and joking around. Desks and chairs of disparate design, size, and color had been forced into rows. They were things that had been picked up here and there. Like the children of this town with their various eye colors and skin tones.

My seat was a low Japanese-style desk of a design very much like the one I had dived under that night. I'd shuddered at the thought that it might actually be the very desk, but I'd soon gotten used to it.

The past was passing. So the terror would disappear at some point too. Right now, I was just sweet little Nako. The teacher apparently thought Yoji was my older brother. That was fine.

Niita took out a pencil and began enthusiastically copying from my notebook. The teacher came in suddenly through the window. This was faster than going around to the actual door, so it wasn't like he was fooling around or anything. Mr. Yu was a surprisingly large man. He was nice and a little weird, with a strange expression like he was always suppressing a laugh. He caught Niita cheating now and said, "Hey now!" but he wasn't threatening at all.

"Now, let's begin. We'll start with Language Arts."

I spread out my copy of the textbook, sat up straight, and stared at the whiteboard.

◆ ◆ ◆

Once evening fell, school was over. A third of the children stayed until the last class. The others disappeared one after another to help with their parents' work or head to their own part-time jobs. So the key lessons were held in the morning. The afternoon was music or art or gym.

Once the students were gone, the janitor would start his rounds. A large man of unknown age with gray skin. In the beginning, I suspected he might have been Bamboo. He didn't work until after sunset, and his gait was exceedingly stiff, like one of the walking dead. But one day, I saw him open his big mouth and scarf down instant *yakisoba* noodles, and I realized with disappointment that he wasn't.

"Quit it!"

I heard Niita shout from the shadow of the prefab classroom. Calling "Niitaaaa," I stretched my neck out and peered in to see the janitor holding Niita's wrist tightly. And pulling down his own pants with his free hand. He looked idiotic, his lower half alone bared to the world. Still half bent over, he glared when he saw me. Maybe this made him loosen his grip on my friend's wrist; Niita twisted and pulled himself free and then ran away as fast as he could. He grabbed my hand, and we fled the scene.

The evening light painted the town red. And with the setting of the sun, it was a lot colder out. Off in the distance, a crow cawed.

"What was that?" I asked.

"A regular grown-up," came the cold response.

I was dumbfounded. "What? Regular?"

"Yeah. But! As if I'd let him do anything for free!" Niita was seriously angry. "I have a price. Mama makes sure to set one. Changing it in line with what the market will bear. He's a thief. Well, I'm not gonna be stolen!"

As I ran along with him, I learned one more thing about this town. That I had to get out. That I had to fight if I was going to live. Even still…

Niita's face in profile as he ran alongside me was dark and tense, like those of the organization men I had seen from beneath the desk that night in the mansion. Impassive like a rusted grown-up.

The evening sun sank above us. It was so heavy I closed my eyes.

✦ ✦ ✦

"Kyo! Hon! Over here!"

I headed down along the beach, all signs of people and houses gradually disappearing, before I finally arrived at the house.

The instant I stepped onto the worn wooden deck,

Mustah called out to me from inside. The smile on his face was almost dazzling. His laughter made his thick hair move like a separate living creature on his head. Jumping up and down, he invited me over with a hand.

Yoji emerged from inside the small room and looked at me, also grinning.

Like a dog called by its master, I raced across the deck and flew into the room. My pigtails swung around and hit my shoulders. "What?"

"Wow! Your hair's getting so long," Mustah said, looking delighted.

Well, that was true, but what did it matter exactly? I cocked my head to one side, and a large hand reached out to stroke my head roughly. My head bent even farther to one side, threatening to snap off. Seeing my troubled look, Yoji burst out laughing. His snickering voice sounded warm and cozy.

"It's not just your hair, either. Right, Yoji?"

"Right!"

"You're taller too, Kyo."

"Am I? I can't tell." As I spoke, they pushed me over to a pillar in the living room.

"Stand up taller! C'mon, give it some oomph!" they urged, excitedly. Mustah gouged out a mark with a utility knife right above my head on the pillar.

The three of us pressed our foreheads together and stared at it intently. Silence.

Yoji made a sound in his throat like a contented cat. Mustah laughed boisterously and praised me for some reason. "You did it," "Nice work," that kind of stuff.

"You're being weird," I said, and finally burst out laughing too.

The mark was six or seven centimeters higher than the one from when I first came to this house by the sea. I was steadily getting taller. Now that I thought about it, the black skirt had been fairly long, but it was actually getting pretty short. We had replaced the blouse twice already too.

Yoji grabbed my hand. Mustah continued to pat my head roughly. They chattered excitedly above me.

"His hair's longer."

"Yeah. And he just keeps growing."

"He's all tanned—he looks so healthy now."

"And he's getting cheekier and cheekier!"

"He's changing every day, isn't he? People grow up."

"It's 'cause he's alive. Not like us. This kid's alive!"

"Fire. This is fire!"

"Fire!"

…Fire?

The flames of countless candles burned in the candlesticks set out around the room. Blowing in from outside, the wind made them all flicker uneasily. The night had only just started, so the candles were still long. But as time passed, they would get shorter, bit by bit. And then, around the time that the night was ending, they would quiver abruptly and go out. The same thing happened every night. Maybe the Bamboo thought that this was what being alive was.

Showered in praise, I felt a little giddy. Their jobs didn't pay a lot, and the blood packs they needed were expensive, so Mustah and Yoji didn't have many luxuries in their lives. They lived modestly. Still, as much as they could, they worried about me and kept me safe. I knew kids living with their human parents who didn't get the chance to study for their future, since their hands were full with the job of turning physical labor or humiliation into money every day. Like my friend Niita.

I was a blessed child. My close brush with death was only a bad dream, but my saviors were real. Was their fierce joy born from the fact that I was alive?

But from my perspective, Yoji—moved to tears by books of poetry—and Mustah—laughing loudly with his camera at the ready, constantly fooling around, hugging me with every muscle in his body—were alive just like me. Even if their hair and nails didn't grow a single millimeter, even if they never got older, they were alive. Which meant…?

Did I think that it meant their hearts pumped? Did I feel like Mustah and Yoji were changing? Flames themselves, growing warmer, flaring out, and then sputtering and dying. I wondered.

At any rate, we unfortunately didn't get to spend a long time talking intimately like this, human me and the Bamboo Mustah and Yoji. That night, again, it was getting to be time for them to head off to work. They fussed unconsciously with each other's hair, pulled up their collars, and inspected appearances before nodding impassively at each other. The whole time, it was like a ritual. I somehow started to feel like it was too bad that I would never take part in this camaraderie.

Abruptly, I found the whole thing weird. One night, I asked Mustah, "Hey, do Bamboo all live in groups of two or three? And if they do, do they all groom one another like that? Forever?"

"Nah, a lot of Bamboo live alone." Mustah shrugged. Lightly, as if to say that was a tragedy that would absolutely never happen to him. "You can tell pretty quick which ones are on their own, y'know."

"How?"

"'Cause they're filthy!"

Hearing this, Yoji frowned slightly.

"Like, their hair's all over the place! And they're not so much wearing their clothes as the clothes are just hanging off their bodies. They stand out at the meetings. Like Yoji here—I mean, he was like that when we first met, y'know."

"What?" I replied, surprised. "No way!"

Combed black hair, neatly pressed shirt. That this boy who was neat nearly to the point of neurosis would have ever been dirty...

"So what about you, Mustah?"

"Me?"

"Yeah."

"...I was always like this." Then he got tight-lipped, and I couldn't get him to tell me anything else.

There was no sense of intimacy or love in the hands that reached out to make the other presentable again tonight. In fact, it looked like a silent boxing match. I was sitting on the floor, looking up at them performing this dance, like I did every evening without ever getting bored of it.

Mustah gasped and reached a hand out toward me. Jokingly, he tugged on the collar of my blouse too. I was secretly delighted, but at the same time, it made my heart hurt for some reason. Like I alone was different.

Right, my Bamboo?

✦ ✦ ✦

That night.

After they left for the night shift, I sat on the floor by myself and spread out my copied textbook pages. I had read all of them so many times that I had almost memorized them.

I was resisting. With help from the mysterious Bamboo. Facing forward, walking straight ahead. But sometimes, those wide-open eyes would swoop down at me. When I let my guard down, the nightmare would descend from the town above. Like when I'd be running around with Niita and the others. And they'd be all, "No girl runs that fast," "How come you can run like that, huh?" Comments like those practically made me jump out of my skin.

I looked up from the textbook pages and stood up. Despite the fact that it was summer, a chill hung in the room, the candles flickering in all kinds of different candlesticks.

As if called to it, I went into the small room. I pushed the lid of the large chest up and stealthily slipped inside. A white fog instantly coiled around me. Cold like the inside of a refrigerator. Seen from inside the chest, the dark ceiling was infinitely far off, and the real world seemed somewhere off in the distance. It was almost like I was dead. Or like I had become the roots of a plant, buried deep within the earth.

I slowly closed my eyes. My lips twitched.

Bamboo. The ones who walk the night. Grass monsters from the depths of China.

I opened my eyes with a gasp. I was shivering inside the chest. Perhaps because of the cold.

I hurriedly crawled out and carefully closed the lid so they wouldn't find out what I'd been up to. I returned to where my papers lay spread out on the living room table.

The summer-night breeze twisted itself around me once more, and my body temperature returned to normal. I solved the math problems. My fingers numb with cold gradually warmed up. The candles crackled.

✦ ✦ ✦

"Anyway, you can't go out tonight. Hey! Are you listening, Kyo? Stray Bamboo are always prowling around on meeting night. Although, actually, this area at night is pretty much totally unsafe all the time. Hey! Mustah, tell him."

"Why should we both tell him the same thing? I'd just look like an idiot for saying it second. No thanks."

"Because he listens to you. Kyo likes you better, Mustah. I mean, he's always going on with that 'My Bamboo, my Bamboo' business. I'm sure he loves you more than anything else in this world."

Mustah felt silent, embarrassed, and scratched his head. "Stay," he growled. "In the house!"

"…Whatever!"

"Hey, Yoji. The kid's not listening to me, like, at all, is he? He's been pretty snarky with us lately, y'know."

"Probably just a rebellious phase? I'm pretty sure I heard humans get sick like that… Mustah, how was it for you?"

"I don't remember!"

The two Bamboo griped and shouted as hands shot out to arrange the other's hair and clothing, the nightly choreographed fight. This ritual of theirs, so quiet and functional when I first saw it, had grown quite animated, a heated exchange of opinions on child-rearing.

I suppressed a laugh and slowly brought my eyes back to the world history reference book opened up on the table. It was actually more along the lines of what they studied in high school. Mr. Yu had lent it to me. Maybe he had even gone to the trouble of buying it with his own money. But he'd skittered away like he always did when I went to thank him. He'd also asked me if I was interested in applying for scholarships and going on to high school. But I'd told him I would ask my guardian, and that had been the end of it.

My appearance had changed a lot already. I never cut my hair, so it had grown all the way to my waist. Maybe through some gene I had inherited from Mama, it was a brownish black with ends that twisted like I'd gotten a perm.

Yoji apparently took comfort in the idea that no one would discover I was a boy if my hair was this long; he said it was okay for me not to wear a skirt. So when my T-shirt or sweater had a girlish design, I got to wear jeans on my bottom half.

With each passing day, Yoji turned into more of a worry-wart, while Mustah spoiled me in equal measure. The three of us found our balance like this.

"Where's the meeting?"

"Can't tell humans."

"Tch! So I don't get to be part of the group…"

"Ha ha ha!"

I was being serious, half-disappointed, but Mustah laughed like it was the funniest thing I'd ever said. Yoji also suppressed a laugh, like he was faced with a pouting child.

"What? What's with you two?"

"Telling anyone other than a Bamboo the time or place of the meeting is against the rules. Our laws are fairly strict."

"Will you end up buried in a hole?"

"No, they wouldn't go that far, but still." Yoji shrugged lightly. "They'd cut an arm off."

"…Would it grow back?"

"It would not."

I shuddered and decided I was definitely giving up on asking about the meeting place. I imagined an arm from Mustah and one from Yoji dropping to the floor with a pair of thuds. The scent of bamboo would puff up, but because they weren't built like humans, the fallen arms would instantly dry up and turn to dust, to be carried away on the wind. A chill ran up my spine, and I shook my head.

"Oh," I said. "But what's a stray Bamboo?"

"Some of 'em don't take the meetings seriously! Mostly the ones who live on their own, y'know? I think it's not like they're extremists, all antigovernment or something, but more like they think the whole thing's just a hassle. Anarchists, I guess? But there aren't any other Bamboo in town on meeting nights, so there's some guys who take advantage and do bad stuff to humans. Only sometimes, but still."

I looked up, pencil wedged beneath my nose. I figured Mustah was more of the hassle type, which made me wonder at how he seemed not to like the anarchist Bamboo.

"Well, if a Bamboo starts going around killing humans,

the government'll find them and make sure to drive them out of town. And the people who go after them are professionals. A murderer's got no chance of avoiding exile. Eventually, that Bamboo'll get sixty years in a barrel in the ground."

"That doesn't bring the dead person back, though." Mustah's voice was dark. And then he looked back at me. "That's why, Kyo, babe. You seriously cannot go out on the night of the full moon."

"Okay."

"Hey, you hear me? Ever since you started going out wandering around at night, we've been worried, y'know!"

"I told you, I'm just meeting friends. Everyone has to work, so we basically can't hang out until evening, okay?"

"What kind of work?"

"Package handling down at the port, a little laundry, some prostitution."

They both looked back at me at the same time, mouths open, ready to speak. Then they looked at each other and clamped them shut again. And then they floated up from the floor and flew out with a whoosh.

For some reason, on meeting nights, Yoji would always have a big red hat on him. Mustah had nothing.

Once they were out on the deck, they locked the door from outside, looking stern. I hurriedly stood up and protested— "C'mon! Again?!"—my long hair swinging from side to side. Yoji feigned ignorance and flew up into the sky. Mustah looked at me, clapped his palms together, pressed the back of his hand to his cheek, telling me to be good and go to bed.

I started to sulk. *Tch!* How long were they going to treat me like a child?

Spinning as he headed upward with his shaky, dangerous style of flying, Mustah's figure vanished in the blink of an eye.

◆ ◆ ◆

I guess the Bamboo hadn't noticed yet that there was an exit hidden behind all the stuff piled up in the kitchen. I took down one box after another and opened the small kitchen door.

The autumn sky was dull, the color of muddy water. The moon was hazy too.

I threw my arms up and stretched for all I was worth. The overprotective grass monsters had finally left me alone! I kicked at the ground with my sneakers, then ran along the deserted, unpaved road hugging the coast. Ruts from wheels were dug out of the pebble-strewn surface. The night of the Bamboo meeting meant the night of a wonderful full moon, and because I was really a boy, of course, I raced through the night, practically exploding with energy.

"Yer late, Nako!"

"Yeah, my brother wouldn't shut up, you know?"

"Well, yeah, he's prob'ly worried about his adorable baby sister going out at night."

I looked down at my own body. "That's not it."

"Huh? What?"

"Nah, it's nothing."

Niita's room. In a run-down place in the center of town where shacks were clustered together.

Niita had basically stopped coming to school. Over half

of the people in my class had vanished from the classroom. In the small room, with four three-tiered beds against the walls, those former classmates gathered like ghosts.

I sat down on a bottom bunk and pulled a reference book from my black leather bag. "Let's do world history."

"I'm with Nako. I mean, we need math the most, but it's also super boring, y'know? Once a month's enough of that."

"We'll get right to it," I said. "This is a world map. Japan is this long, thin island."

"Whoa! It's tiny!"

"This is China."

"It's huge! So big!"

"My parents are from Argentina."

"Um, this is their homeland then."

"Really? Isn't that too far away?"

We met like this sometimes after night fell so I could teach them what I'd learned in school. I picked things people needed to actually live in the world and offered up awkward lectures. Like math and accounting and English and geography.

Mustah and Yoji didn't know about these nighttime lessons, but Mr. Yu had probably figured it out. He'd sometimes ask me how everyone was. Each time, I'd answer briefly, *Good.*

Everyone pushed and shoved and jostled to peer at the world map. The balance of power and the state of trade between countries. Religious beliefs and ethnic issues. As I related various facts and concepts, Niita and the others would say that, now that I mentioned it, a customer from this ethnic group had been like this, or that such-and-such kind of cargo had come to the port recently.

"You know that janitor guy?" Niita said, suddenly. It was right around the time the conversation was petering out and we were opening the candy drops someone had brought.

I remembered him yanking on Niita's arm, naked from the waist down, and I frowned as I nodded.

"Turns out he's actually the same age as Mr. Yu." Niita was casual.

"Noooo way. He's so old, though."

"It's true, though! I guess they were kids together in school. And on top of that, the old man was actually smarter or something."

It felt like the air had suddenly got thinner. I wondered what it was.

"But he couldn't go to high school or anything, so he started working, y'know? And then he didn't have any money, and he was stuck here. And in this place, even if you don't start out garbage, you turn into garbage. So basically, he ended up like that. I guess he asked Mr. Yu for that job as the janitor."

"Is that what happened." There was a hard edge to my voice.

Niita slowly lifted his face. He looked right into my eyes, something he didn't usually do. "Nako, don't you end up like that."

"Come on! What's that, out of the blue! There's no way I would. A total pervert like that. Quit it!" I leaned forward resolutely.

The other guys were also surprised, wondering what this was about, and they looked at Niita. His face was incredibly serious.

"I'll always be on your side. Okay? You just keep being our Miss Nako, our teacher. I like you and all, but I never feel like I *like you* like you, you know? But anyway, you're a good kid, like you were brought up right. And, like, you make my head spin. So it's like, you know."

"I know what? You're creeping me out, Niita."

"If you grow up and turn into garbage, then there'll be nothing for me to believe in in this town."

✦ ✦ ✦

Niita walked me to the meandering road that ran along the coast. I badly missed the time when he had sat beside me in the slanting prefab school that was a school in name only. It'd only been a couple of years since then, but all kinds of things had changed.

Niita waved his hand vigorously and then went back the way we had come. Alone, I started running toward the house, the moon full in the sky. The autumn wind was already cool. I shivered. All I could hear was the sound of my own feet. Orange sneakers. I was getting pretty tired. Somewhere, a cat meowed. Gradually, I slowed down to a walk.

And then, suddenly, I heard a sound from somewhere—ominous, like something slicing through the air. I gasped and turned around.

I don't know if it came from behind or hurled itself from the side. A shadow much larger than I was hung over me, and before I knew it, I was on the ground. My first thought was that it was a stray Bamboo. I was wrong.

My shirt was immediately ripped open. My jeans were

yanked down. My sneakers sailed through the air a surprisingly long distance. *Ah! He thinks I'm a girl.*

I came back to myself and tried to scream. Instantly, a thick mitt of a hand clamped down over my mouth. *I can't breathe!* My eyeballs were on the verge of popping out of my skull. I spasmed violently. I reached out and grabbed my attacker's wrist. But he didn't even flinch.

The hazy moon swelled up. The night grew eerily deeper. My consciousness started to fade. All the strength drained from my limbs. I was basically naked by this point. But the man couldn't get my jeans to come off and was visibly annoyed. He pulled out a knife and cut into the fabric. The blade hit my thigh and dug into my skin. He pulled it back and brandished it, nicking my chest. The scent of blood spread out around us.

I didn't have enough air. A weird noise came from my throat. Maybe I was going to die. This suddenly. Even though I had just been laughing and having fun with my friends.

Then I saw a black shadow closing in on me, obstructing the large moon. Eyes I had started to close opened wide in surprise. Relieved tears welled up in the corners. The face of a young man with dark skin filled my blurry field of view.

Mustah!

I had a dream like this once.

In the next instant, the man hanging over me flew off to one side. Lightly, like a scrap of fabric. I tried to say something, but my throat could only produce a weak croak.

The knife the man still clutched grazed Mustah's cheek, making the faintest of sounds. *Shf!* A straight line appeared on Mustah's cheek, and the green smell of grass unfurled around us. Liquid—I couldn't tell if it was red or green or clear—fell from the wound and landed with a splat on my chest, atop my own wound, making my chest throb painfully for some reason.

The wound on Mustah's cheek closed like magic. His beautiful skin was unblemished again. It was like watching a video in rewind.

I heard Yoji's sharp cry. In the blink of an eye, he was standing beside me. He was pointing at me and shouting shrilly—so very different from the usual gentle, calm Yoji.

Hazily, I looked down to see what he was pointing at. The nick on my chest from the knife, red blood oozing from it. And the liquid from Mustah's cheek slowly melting into it, illuminated by the light of the moon. Gently.

✦ ✦ ✦

"Yoji! Yoji! Yoji!"

"Shout all you want—it's not going to change anything. Mustah, bring Kyo over here. Hurry."

"Ah…ah…unh." I had my hands full with breathing, now that I was finally able to again. I eagerly gulped down fresh air, my throat wheezing.

Mustah timidly stepped forward and easily picked me up. Me, half-naked and covered in blood. In too much of a panic, he flew up high in the night sky, spinning around in place and descending abruptly to bring me over to the deserted lot to one side. Finally, he lowered me to the ground.

Yoji peered into my eyes. "How do you feel right now?"

"Um. I'm getting cold. And I feel kinda weird, I guess."

Next to me, Mustah groaned. But what exactly was all this? I mean, the hoodlum was gone now, and neither of the cuts he'd given me qualified as lethal.

Yoji bared his teeth. His appearance suddenly changed completely. *This* was the face of a ferocious, supernatural monster that walked the night. He put his lips to my bared chest. I twitched and reflexively pulled back as Yoji licked at the cut. Mustah was silent, still panicked. Yoji sucked up the blood oozing from my wound.

"Unh!"

"Just hang on, Kyo. Okay?" Mustah said, sounding like he was about to burst into tears. He kneaded his hands together restlessly, his face crumpled up.

Yoji lifted his head and spat out blood. And then he brought his lips back down. Suck it up, spit it out. And again and again.

I began to fade from consciousness.

"Kyo, you okay?" Mustah hung his head. "Sorry, okay? Sorry."

"What? Is…"

"And Yoji, you too! I'm sorry!"

"You don't need to apologize, Mustah. It's finished now." Yoji lifted his head again. His lips were dyed red with my blood. This, along with his pale skin, made him look he had been made up for his own funeral.

"Yoji, that's some nice work there. If it was me, I'd just keep drinking. And then I'd actually kill Kyo…"

"We've just had different experience as Bamboo, that's all," Yoji said, lightly, his face still covered in blood. "You only know seventeen or so years of Bamboo life, right? But I witnessed the war and the revolution. I've seen a lot of history. And I was Bamboo the whole time."

I had no idea what he was talking about. For the first time in a long time, I remembered the tearstained book of Chinese poetry. Idly, I wondered if Yoji was one of the Bamboo who had come flowing down an eternal river from a distant foreign land.

The moon suddenly became very blurry. And then I passed out.

+ + +

The next thing I knew, I was back at the house.

Mustah had probably flown home with me in his arms again. Like the first time he'd brought me to this house. What was different this time, though, was that now his face was drained of all color, and he was silently clutching my hand. He wasn't threatening me either; no *Quit fooling around, you brat, I'll eat you up like jam* or anything.

As for Yoji, he went out and came back again carrying a pile of straw rope for some reason. His face was tenser than I'd ever seen it. He wound the rope around me and tied me to a pillar.

"Poor thing. Our little Kyo…"

"It'd be a real problem if something happened during the day. We wouldn't be able to protect him."

"Yeah. But—aah, I really am so sorry, Kyo!"

Sorry, he says. *If something happened*, he says. What?

The two grass monsters sat still by my side, both silent, until moments before dawn. Only the flames of the candles moved. And then they headed to the small room, looking back regretfully, and climbed into the chest. The lid slowly closed, and I was alone in the living room.

The morning sun began to shine on the other side of the glass doors. The sea also shone whitely, announcing the start of a new day.

I closed my eyes, and the afterimage of the morning was on the backs of my eyelids. It was maybe the first time I'd ever gone to sleep at this hour, I thought, and in the next instant, I lost consciousness. Wrapped in light, I slept.

◆ ◆ ◆

In the evening, someone came to visit. I thought it might have been Mr. Yu. It was unusual for sweet little Nako to miss school, so maybe he was worried about me. Kind Mr. Yu, always pretending he didn't care, was in reality a worry-wart.

"Hallo!" came a forlorn voice. It *was* Mr. Yu. "Nako?" How weak it sounded. "Come back to school. Come tomorrow… I mean, how could you stop just like that? Your teacher here's had enough of that. All you kids, you just disappear… No matter what I teach you… That it should all be in vain… It's not! Halloooo!"

And then, just when I thought he'd gone, he continued, "Think about the scholarship. I'll sit down and talk to your brother!"

Right. Mr. Yu had checked into a scholarship for me so that I could go on to high school. But I had kind of put off talking about it with Mustah and Yoji.

No one came out to welcome him in, so after a while, Mr.

Yu gave up and went home. No doubt he would have been shocked to find out his student was tied up with straw rope behind the sofa.

Mr. Yu… Yoji. Hey, Mustah…

I drifted off to sleep again.

Around the time the sun was starting to go down, I woke up again. My mind, which had been filled with cotton since last night, was finally crystal clear. I couldn't sit up or stand, but I moved my head back and forth and took some deep breaths. Outside, the sea twisted gently.

Just as I thought, *Aah, the sun's setting*, I heard a loud bang. I looked back and saw the lid of the chest in the center of the small room popping up, exploding outward. Two faces appeared simultaneously above the side of the chest.

Rather than standing up slowly and gracefully like they usually did, the Bamboo leaped out, pushing and shoving at each other, panicked. Yoji leaped in my direction, but he overshot, missing me by quite a bit, while Mustah flew up and slammed his head against the ceiling, like a bird that had somehow gotten into a human house.

Finally, two sets of eyes peered at me from either side. The Bamboo held their breath.

I looked back at them in confusion. "What?"

They said nothing. With no other choice, I waited.

"Aah, thank God," Yoji sighed, eventually.

"Yeah! You're not a Bamboo! Honestly, goddammit! I—aah, you did it, Kyo!" Nothing Mustah said as he roughly wrapped his arms around me made a lick of sense. His beard stabbed my cheek painfully. The thick scent of bamboo filled my nostrils. The ticking of the wall clock seemed excessively loud.

They looked at each other and nodded slowly.

"The flame's not out!"

"Mm. Thank God. I thought I'd maybe put it out by accident. Like I'd done something I couldn't take back. But I was wrong. The flame's still here!"

"Kyo! Aah, this is just great, Kyo!"

My mind grew even clearer. "What do you mean, I'm not a Bamboo?" I asked as they finally untied me, my voice slightly hard.

They looked at me together, expressionless. Their eyes glowed eerily with a glittering chill, utterly inhuman.

✦ ✦ ✦

"So, with Bamboo, you see? Some Bamboo were born Bamboo, and then there are the Bamboo who were once human, who got turned into Bamboo," said Yoji. "I've been a Bamboo ever since I was born. I've seen a lot of history, albeit from deep in the mountains. If I told you my real age, I'm sure you wouldn't believe me. When I came to Japan from China, I changed my name and everything else to start a new life."

"And I was born a human and got turned into a Bamboo. There's a whole bunch of stuff I'm still not quite used to. That's why I'm so stupid and slow. *Tch!*" said Mustah.

"How does a person become a Bamboo?"

"It's a blood infection."

"So that's why, okay? Something like yesterday was so dangerous. If human blood and our blood… Well, that liquid, if they mix, you turn into a Bamboo. And once that happens, you're stuck being a miserable creature that lives on blood and can only go out at night. And that's the end of your growth too—middle school for a century. It's an existence without a flame. So that was seriously a close call, y'know."

"I sucked out the blood before it could circulate through your body," Yoji said. "Well, I've been around for a while, so I just sort of knew."

"But, Kyo, hon, are you really okay?" Mustah asked. "You do look pale, actually."

I was sitting quietly on the sofa, listening to Mustah and Yoji seated on either side of me. Yoji was holding my hand, while Mustah had a hand on the nape of my neck. They were super overprotective and treated me too much like a child, but for tonight at least, there was probably nothing I could do about it.

My feelings were complicated after finding out that I had just barely avoided being transformed into a Bamboo. Even I didn't how exactly I felt. Was it fear? Or...

"Mustah, what happened to you?"

"I was almost dead. It was either die or be a Bamboo. So I became a Bamboo."

"Back then, I came to Japan as an immigrant. I was alone, and I guess I was pretty dirty looking. So people stayed away from me. And I could hardly get any real work," Yoji said.

"This one night, I was racing along on my motorcycle, delivering kebabs, when I happened to run into some thugs from some organization up on the hill. Stray bullet hits my carotid artery." Mustah pointed to the side of his neck. "That was that, y'know?"

"I found him, though," Yoji said. "The scent of blood lured me in. But we have a rule that you can only eat the dead, so I couldn't drink his blood until he'd died. So I was just waiting politely."

"Like, for me to die completely. What a creep, huh!"

"No, it's just nature."

"But I guess he changed his mind all of sudden. Like, he looked into my eyes and saw something that made him think, 'Oh ho! Maybe I could get along with this guy.'"

"He was dying, but he looks up at me and says, 'Wash your face. It's filthy!' and laughs. And then I realized with a gasp that that was why I couldn't get a job, why no one would come near me, why I was alone," Yoji said.

"So he decided to make me his comrade. He infected me. And then he locked me up the first day, y'know? Because I'd get crazed. And it's true—all your organs and everything in your body change. It's impossibly painful. But I guess it was a fair bit better than dying like a dog on the side of the road."

"And then, once it was the two of us, I found work right away. Maybe because I had someone to groom me, to clean me up," Yoji said. "Well, I still have to change jobs every few years or so, since I don't visibly age. But it's a peaceful life. To the point where you have to wonder if it's actually a good thing."

"Because you won't die, no matter what happens."

"Right. But that's because there's no flame. So it won't go out," Yoji said.

Having said that, Yoji and Mustah looked at each other. A sad silence rolled by. No, more than sad—regretful. Like they couldn't completely accept the fact that there was no flame.

Yoji stroked my head. Mustah squeezed my hand.

Even as I thought it was maybe weird to say it now, my

teacher's voice came back to life in my ears. "Um, hey?" I said suddenly. "Can I go to high school?"

They both stared at me blankly, so my voice got smaller.

"I-I was going to say something, you know, but… Mr. Yu checked out scholarships for me. Told me to ask my brother. I mean…anyway, it's still next year, but…"

The expressions on their faces slowly softened.

"What? You're going to study, take the entrance exam, go to high school? Amazing!"

"And then you'll be all grown-up, and you'll take the exam for employment somewhere and be a full member of society? You? But you were so little! Aah, really?"

"What? So…it's okay?"

The two of them stood and held hands. And then they looked down on me and, almost overcome with emotion, said, "Of course it's okay. Thank you, Kyo!"

"Huh?"

"Do you have any idea how happy we are that you're so filled with hope, so bright, so healthy? How delightful every day is?" said Yoji.

"Okay, now you're being over-the-top. Right, Mustah?" I looked up toward the other Bamboo. His lips were also pulled tightly together, and his eyes glittered with something like tears. "C'mon, even you, Mustah?"

"Aah, you just keep getting bigger, huh, Kyo! Already in high school next year! You really—y'know, you're growing up so fast, you're so adorable."

"Come on…"

Their smiling faces were dazzling, entirely free of shadow. So I smiled back, albeit bewilderedly. Beyond the glass windows, the sea rolled in and pushed back out, and rolled in again.

Mustah said he wanted to measure my height and led me over to the pillar. He held the ruler up and made a mark. "Whoa! You grew almost another whole centimeter!"

Delighted, Yoji came over. "Kyo, maybe you—you might end up being a real beanpole. I don't know what we'll do if you get even bigger than we are!"

"As if!"

The pair exploded with laughter.

The ocean twisted gently on the other side of the window. The lazy breeze seemed soft, and everything looked serene. The flames of the candles, now fairly small, flickered quietly.

FAIR

"Kyo. Kyo, hon! Come on! Wake up!"

"Ah!"

"It's morning, sleepyhead!" Yoji said in his kind voice, and then Mustah got in on the act by poking me, so I hurriedly yanked myself up.

The breaking dawn on the other side of the window burned red. Inside the room, the flickering flames of the candles on their candlesticks were so small they looked like they would go out at any second.

I suddenly remembered the night when, in that very place, I'd rejoiced with the two Bamboo that I hadn't been infected with Mustah's blood. It still seemed like yesterday, despite the time that had passed since then.

When I got up from the sofa, Yoji was putting blood packs into the large refrigerator. Mustah took the old camera down from the bookshelf and fooled around with taking my picture while I was still foggy headed. I grumbled to myself, but I couldn't be angry when I saw that cloudless smile. Quietly shrugging to myself, I went to wash my face. Lately, the pair annoyed me in the way of adorable children who never shut up.

I changed into my uniform—my high school blazer and pleated navy skirt. It was getting chillier these days, so I wrapped a scarf around my neck too. A cute one with a heart pattern to make Yoji relax. Pulled back my brown hair in a ponytail. It really was long like a horse's tail, and the ends curled up and around.

By the time I returned to the living room, they were already gone. Turning around, I saw the lid of the chest in the middle of the small room slowly being lowered.

"Okay, I'm off then!" I said, just in case.

"Okay! Good night!"

"Don't forget to take your breakfast with you, Kyo!" came Yoji's voice.

And then Mustah spoke, sounding dissatisfied. "And what do you hope to get out of making him any bigger than he already is? Kyo's head is going to go right through the roof…"

Their giggling voices receded and then disappeared completely when the lid came down, leaving behind nothing but a faint white fog. The sense of something else alive in the house abruptly vanished.

I turned on my heel, picked up my heavy bag, and went out the door. Dawn.

Outside the house was a vintage scooter. Not a single one of the students in the high school in the town above was broke enough to be forced to ride a machine like this, but it didn't really bother me. The custom job Mustah had done on it was perfect, so the thing ran well, at any rate. I set out, riding roughly on the pockmarked road along the coast at daybreak. My shining future was just up ahead.

I climbed the hill. When I went around the curves, the bike and I both listed to one side. My eyes ran over the people of the lower town who were out on the job already, one after another. Delivery. Construction. I often spotted children mixed in among them. I'm sure my old friends were in there somewhere too. But we hadn't talked in a long time; I wouldn't have noticed them in that crowd. And I mean, from their side, in my uniform I would have looked like nothing other than one of the high school students from above that they always saw.

I pursed my lips and abruptly remembered something Mr. Yu had told me. *Nako, it would be great if you went to high school, studied hard, and then got to go on to higher education. It'd really open up your future options. You'd have a real stable life waiting for you then.*

And I want to give you the help you need, he'd continued, with something like a sigh. *I don't want to see any more talented kids trapped in dead ends. I used to be a helpless little kid once too, but I'm a teacher now, so I should be able to prevent at least a few of those hard destinies.*

As I approached the town above, the streets started to change. High-class mansions and broad roads like a theme park. There was almost no one out working at that hour.

I drew closer to the school. I could see the cross rising

up. Housed in a building that at first glance looked like a church, the Korean-funded school was Christian. I raced onto school grounds, the engine roaring like the machine was angry. I dashed into the library through the back entrance, took my seat, and opened my textbook. I had always been good at slipping in through the kitchen door or sneaking in through a back entrance.

I got right down to studying. Above all else, a scholarship student needed to have grades that were far and away superior to any rivals in the same grade. And that applied double if you wanted another scholarship to go on to university. If you were burning with ambition, you had to put in the effort.

I had never expected to return to the town above in this form. But seeing the person I was now, no one would connect me with the boy who had disappeared without a trace from the organization's tight grip that night long ago.

Hymns wafted down to me from the school chapel, and I unconsciously started humming along, joining my voice with those of the singers, who were so certain of the love God had for them. Eventually, I twisted the words into blasphemous lyrics that fit neatly with the song to accompany the melody.

Dear Lord of this town. I survived. A miracle. And I came back here. Can you see me? Or maybe you've long since forgotten the events of that night, you shitheel of a god?

✦ ✦ ✦

During class, my head stuck out above the others since I was taller than even the boys. But no one suspected that this girl was actually a boy. It was a strange thing.

A few of the girls could have been called cute, but that was basically as far as it went for me. Maybe I didn't really have time for that. I desperately followed the characters as they were spelled out on the blackboard.

After class, I worked part-time in a cozy, expensive cake shop. Yoji had reacted with "Someone might find you!" but Mustah had had my back. Scratching his bearded chin, he'd said, "Whoa, whoa, take a look at him, though. Does this look like the same Kyo from back then? He's about five times as tall. And he's a girl, y'know? Plus, if he gets a job down here, we'll never stop worrying about his safety."

As always, they were both overprotective. And even though they were just barely making ends meet, they absolutely refused to take the money I made at my job. They went and made "Little Kyo's Piggy Bank" and tucked every bit of it away for me.

Around the time the sun was setting, I changed back into my school uniform and headed back down to the town below. I sped up as I descended the hill. It was cold out. As forward-looking and hardworking as I was, I loved danger and thrills for some reason. So I didn't let up on the accelerator, not even on the curves.

"Nako!"

When I had gone around the ninth curve, a skinny man jumped out from the side of the plant where they canned the fish brought into the port. This was where they made the cans that Yoji often brought home for me. I nearly ran the man down but managed to come to a screeching stop.

Black, tanned from the sun, eyes sunken. Only when I peered into those black eyes did I finally realize I was looking at one of my friends from that old prefab school. I didn't jump off the scooter but stayed as I was with my hands on the handlebars. If I let my guard down just because it was someone I knew, I could get punched or have my money or even my scooter stolen. You had to steel yourself, or you'd die pretty quick down here.

For a second, the boy looked like he'd taken a punch to the nose at this wariness from an old friend. He held his tongue regretfully. And then, "Mr. Yu died."

"Huh?" My voice was high.

The boy went ahead and straddled the back of the scooter without asking. As if he'd completely forgotten that the world we lived in had changed and I had been afraid of him only seconds earlier. He wrapped his skinny arms around my waist.

"Last night! Stabbed on the road near the school. They said his wallet was missing! Even though there couldn't have been much in it, eh? It was too late when they found him, just a bit ago. He was thrown onto the side of the road like a piece of garbage."

"Mr. Yu…" I repeated. I heard my voice trembling. "Hey, where's Niita?" Now that I thought about it, I hadn't seen him in ages. My best friend when I was a kid.

I got a sigh from behind. "So, like, I dunno, right? I guess he's going all over the place to make a buck. When I saw him last month, he said his price had dropped since he got bigger, and it was tough going. 'Cause everyone wants kids. I thought about getting him to tell you or something, but no one knows where he is now. That's why I was waiting for you, Nako. Here."

"You were, huh? Thanks!"

"No big. Anyway, they took Mr. Yu back to his house already. His mom and dad're crying like crazy. His old students are going over there too. You know where his place is?"

Of course I knew. Before I started high school, I would go over there to get textbooks and reference books and plain old books. Like a stray dog hopefully visiting the house of someone who fed it. All the time back then. His house was the usual type of shack, with a roof and walls that just barely kept the wind and rain out.

I gripped the handlebars tightly. Engine humming, I started out again. The wind blew at my skirt.

"Whoa, Nako!" the boy cried out. "Your skirt! People'll see your legs!" He reached out a hand to try to pull it back down. Even though they were just boys' legs.

I said nothing and accelerated. My driving became dangerous.

"Nako, don't cry!" I heard from behind me. "I mean, crying's not gonna bring Mr. Yu back. He's gone, you know. Somewhere far away. To a peaceful sky."

The evening sun chased us from behind. The red light of a sun setting like a sob.

◆ ◆ ◆

"Kyo! You're late. We were worr—Kyo?"

Yoji and Mustah came out to meet me when I arrived home around the time the sun had set completely. My eyes were swollen from crying. They had been standing on the patio outside, waiting for me fretfully even though it was well past the time they should have left for work. When I looked up, instead of being properly groomed as usual, their hair and clothes and cuffs were all slightly off.

"Kyo?"

I told them that Mr. Yu was dead, and Yoji gasped. Mustah hugged me silently. I was much taller than they were now. I pressed my face against Mustah's smooth black hair and breathed deeply of the scent of bamboo I loved so much. We stayed like that for a while, and then I pulled away. I reached out and gently fixed Mustah's messy hair with my fingers.

"You're huge, you know," he said, almost blushing.

"I'm alive." These words came out of my mouth instead of the usual laugh. It was too much, and I started weeping again. Yoji came around from behind to stroke my shuddering back.

And then the two of them quietly flew off to the north, where the hospital was. I set myself down on the bench on the patio and saw them off, waving. The surging ocean broke against the shore, then retreated.

The figure of Mr. Yu hopping in through the window, his serious face in profile when he looked into scholarships for me. Whenever I showed my face at his shack, he would lend me books to study, tell me about how there were all kinds of jobs in this world. I remembered how he was large and yet somehow ephemeral, like a shadow puppet. And then the face in death I'd just seen. He would never again think or worry about his students, search for hope together with them. He had gone somewhere far away, by himself. To a peaceful sky.

I curled up on the bench. For the first time in a long time, that day I thought I'd forgotten came charging in from the distant past. My sister. A good person with no sins to be punished for. But she had died cruelly, her hopes and future and dignity all ripped up from the roots. Did it even matter that that had happened? Was that really okay? Did the god of our town occasionally look away?

People died young, especially in this town. Without any particular reason. No matter how amazing the person. Even if they worked hard. Mr. Yu hadn't been given any special treatment as a soul worthy of life. And once you died, you never got to see anyone again. Even the people closest to you—you didn't get to be with them again for even a split second.

I threw my bag as hard as I could. It opened up, and my textbooks and notebooks spilled out. But I couldn't muster the energy to pick them up.

I stood stock-still, shaking, and howled for Mr. Yu and for my sister.

◆ ◆ ◆

Daybreak. The time of day when the echoes of the waves crashing in and receding was at its zenith. Winter was approaching and the days were shorter, so it was still dark outside. Mustah and Yoji came flying home through the night sky.

The sofa, the table, everything in the house was flipped upside down. The place was such a disaster that it was almost surprising it hadn't somehow spontaneously caught fire too. I stood vacantly in the middle of it all.

Still standing where he'd touched down by the window,

Mustah was frozen in place like a Bamboo statue. Yoji slowly came inside in his stead.

"Please." I was trembling all over. It was the first time I'd even spoken to my beloved Bamboo like this. "I'll never ask for anything else. Make me a Bamboo."

"Why on earth would you ask for that, Kyo?" Yoji's voice was very soft. I'd never heard it that soft before. It was at the lower limit of what a person could produce with a voice. My heart throbbed in my chest.

"Because people die." My voice was shaking too.

"Don't you think that's exactly why the fact that you're alive has such serious value, Kyo?"

I shook my head stubbornly from side to side.

Mustah winced, as if in shock. It was like the air itself had shuddered.

"I mean, people just die. No matter how hard you try, how hard you fight, it doesn't mean anything. We can't escape death. Even the most wonderful life ends eventually. And so cruelly on top of that."

"But, you see, Kyo—"

"I mean, me! If I go to school today, I might not make it home again! I could be killed by someone, I could be in an accident!"

"Kyo!"

"If I die, I won't get to see you ever again, Mustah!" I shouted out my true feelings, and then I was running without even realizing it. I wrapped my arms around Mustah, who was slumped lifelessly against the window frame, and hugged him as hard as I could.

He jumped like he'd been burned. Nervous that this fierce

love was perhaps a burden, I tried to pull away. And then he reached his arms out, grabbed my shoulders, and pulled me in closer.

My heart was full of pain and joy. Mustah, so tiny now. My nose hit the top of his head. It broke my heart, filled my heart. My Bamboo. My papa. My friend. My lover. My Bamboo. Mustah.

His mouth was at my neck, his shuddering breath warm on my skin. He was silent for a long time.

When I peered softly at his face, he was staring not at me, but at Yoji with a pleading look. Hurt at the idea that this was troubling for him, I hurriedly pulled away and leaned against the wall, averting my eyes.

Yoji stepped over the many things scattered on the floor and walked with a deliberate step toward me. "You have a flame." His voice still quiet. "Why can't you see the value of that?"

"But it's a fire that goes out so fast! If a strong wind blows… If the candle burns down… So soon…"

"And that's why we love you. We will always love you this deeply."

Don't say that again. I mean, love. Tears poured from my eyes.

"Please don't forget, Kyo, hon."

"Forget what?!"

"We won't steal your fire. We want to protect it."

I suddenly loved him too much, which put me in a truly perverse mood. My words were harsh, directed more toward Mustah that Yoji. "So is it, like, maybe—if you turned a person into a Bamboo, something'll happen to you if they find out? Like they'll punish you by burying you in a barrel or cutting off one of your arms or something? Because the Bamboo rules are strict, right? And you don't want that, right?"

Yoji snorted with laughter at my sulking words. I was startled at the cold look on his face. Afraid that maybe I had really made him mad.

"No, that's not it, Kyo," he said, his voice hushed and even. "In fact, just the opposite. The gravest sin for a Bamboo is not to kill a human being, nor is it to tell them the location of our meetings."

"So what is it then?"

"It's to live with a human being."

I gasped. Unconsciously, I looked back at Mustah. He averted his eyes awkwardly, and with that, I knew it was true.

I remembered the words of the Bamboo man who had come along a very long time ago, when I shook and shivered all alone in a mansion in the town above: *I'd get more than the barrel underground for sixty years for this. I mean, punishment by fire's no joke, y'know? It's pretty much the most painful way for us to disappear from this world. So it's a no-go. Sorry, 'kay?*

The gravest sin? Punishment by fire?

"Bamboo can never tell humans who they really are, and we can absolutely never live with them. I mean, in terms of the bigger picture, it's a danger for the entire tribe. But Mustah and I have kept the flame that you are a secret for almost seven years now. Because this joy is greater than anything else we've known. Rescuing you, helping you grow up, and finally sending you out into the world. Our bodies are cold, and yet our hearts are filled with warmth."

"Send me out?" Yoji suddenly felt very far away. Almost

like a stranger. His voice was cool, his face too devoid of expression. I panicked. "Yoji, what are you talking about? We're going to live together forever, right? The three of us, always, you know? But I'm the only one who's human, so I'll get old. I'm already this tall and all. I'll grow up, I'll get old, and someday, I'll die. You'll be sad. If that kind of goodbye's coming, then don't you think it'd be better to just go ahead and make me a Bamboo too, like just do it?"

"No, I *don't* think so," came the cold voice of refusal.

I looked at Mustah imploringly. But he continued to avert his eyes. His profile was in shadow, and I couldn't read the expression on his face.

"You—that's a lie…"

"No. Right at the start, we made it very clear with each other. We'd raise you properly until you were eighteen."

"Eighteen? Th-that's soon! So then once I'm eighteen… you won't protect me anymore? We can't live together? The two of you won't be with me forever, after all…"

"Please understand." Yoji looked pained. "We care about you more than anything else in this world. We want you to grow up and leave this nest. And you've been living up to our every expectation. You decided yourself to go on to high school. You're fighting every day. All the work you've done, everything you've gotten in return—it's filled our hearts with pride. You can't live in this impoverished town with grass monsters forever. It doesn't suit the wonderful person you've become… That's how it will be in the near future. So, Kyo, hon."

Vrrm! I felt like I heard the humming of the scooter's motor. The winding road I climbed every morning to the town above. I loved these people so much that it sparked a desire, an ambition in me to try to fight, to crawl away from my horrible fate. How could I leave them? It was too awful.

It felt like my heart was being yanked out by an invisible hook. My only thought was of Yoji and Mustah trying to get rid of me. And then they would go back to their carefree life, just the two of them. Close, quiet, for however many decades. Without ever growing older. Without changing either. Sleeping naked, facing each other inside the chilled chest. And then they would gradually forget me. On the other side of deep time.

I couldn't stand it. "Make me a Bamboo too!" I screamed. "If you do it now, there's still time! Please!"

"We can't!"

"But I want to be with you forever. I love you so much it hurts. Both of you...Mustah..."

"We do too. We really understand, Kyo."

"So then—"

"But we can't." Yoji came over to me and set a hand on my shoulder. His face came into view below. Afraid, I turned my eyes away. The gentle echo had returned to his voice. "Our dream is for you to grow up and live. And it doesn't matter a bit if you get busy and naturally forget all this about having lived with some weird grass monsters. Because that is in itself growing up, living and changing."

"Kyo." Mustah's voice came to me from far away. "You understand, yeah?"

"I don't!"

"It's like, I mean, everyone, y'know? They all have a monster or two they were friends with when they were kids. If

they're human, that is. But they all forget, they grow up.
There might be some faithful ones, sometimes, who remember again once they get old. But for the most part, people
get busy, they burn brightly, they live their lives, forever for-
getting. That's..."

*Fire? Is that living? Mustah. Yoji. Liars! As if I'd believe
something like that!*

I thought about coming home to this house one day when
I'd turned eighteen and finding no one there, like no one had
ever been there, like it had been just a long dream. I didn't
think it was a loneliness I could endure. I didn't want that,
I totally didn't want that. *Mustah, don't go away.* I shook my
head, and Yoji slowly held out his hand. His figure standing
there before me threatened to disappear even in that moment,
and I howled sadly like I'd been bitten, sinking to the floor on
the spot.

◆ ◆ ◆

The night of the full moon. Winter had come. The air around
me was frozen, breaking and snapping each time I took a
step. The breath I exhaled was white. The moon was stupidly
bright. I narrowed my eyes and kept walking endlessly.

...How many weeks had passed? Since that night, Yoji
had returned to his usual self. I, however, had become very
quiet, and Mustah had been in a bad mood the whole time.

Ordered to return the disaster of a room to its original
state, I cleaned it up myself. One of Mustah's precious cameras was broken, but he didn't get mad at me in words. In
fact, it was so awkward that neither of us could look the

other in the eye. He acted like he was poking bruised skin whenever we talked, and I choked at coming face-to-face with the Bamboo in the house.

I hadn't actually been going to school since then either. It was like the thread of tension that had kept me working like a dog ever since I came to the lower town had been cut with a neat snip. When I thought about getting on my scooter in the morning, my body stopped moving. I simply couldn't muster the energy to prepare for classes or review or study for exams. The Bamboo couldn't see me during the day, so they hadn't noticed yet. I used that to my advantage and spent my days wandering around.

And tonight in particular, the full moon meant that the Bamboo were at their meeting, so I didn't need to worry about them finding me, no matter how much I noodled around outside. Which was why I was simply walking to nowhere in particular down the frozen coastal road.

I felt like I had seen something move in the shadows. I had walked listlessly to the area where the shacks were most heavily concentrated. People were moving around in rooms here and there, but it wasn't safe outside, so there was basically no one out walking. The shacks were illuminated by the blinding light of the moon.

The movement was followed by a sound from a corner of the ruined remains of one of the shacks. I went over and peered inside to see a mountain of stiff fabric squirming. A person wearing rags. No, two of them. The one on the bottom was a man in work clothes, while the one on top was a person with horribly tangled long hair. I couldn't tell if it was a man or a woman. The arms of the man below were reaching out in my direction, twitching. And then, exhausted of strength, they fell heavily to the ground. Apparently, the person on top was biting his neck. And then that person noticed me and turned around.

It was a woman. Young. She looked about the same age as me. Maybe a girl still in her teens. Her round eyes were dangerous, glittering. Blood was smeared around her mouth.

The face of the man on the ground was in shadow, so I couldn't see it. But blood was oozing from his neck. When I realized, *Ah! This is a Bamboo's meal*, the girl slowly turned up the corners of her bloody mouth. She was smiling.

"Yer pretty good at making yourself invisible."

And my chest throbbed like it was shrinking. So bitter-sweet, those words. Like I was hearing them from the distant past. I smiled like I was about to suddenly cry. "Yeah…I've always been like that."

"What?" The girl blinked. That mischievous expression was also like him.

I suddenly felt close to her. "So you're Bamboo then."

"You know about us?"

"Walkers of the nights! Drinkers of human blood! You eat living flesh!"

"That's about it." The girl smiled again. "You sure know a lot, huh?"

I looked her over carefully. Her pale face was filthy with dust and dirt. Her neck and arms were also jet-black, and she was wearing layers of rags that looked like they'd been thrown away. Even in the town down here, known for its poverty, it was rare to see someone this destitute. Especially a young woman.

And then the bloody mouth. The palms of her hands were red too.

A stray Bamboo then. All alone, she couldn't groom herself because she didn't show up in mirrors, so she'd gotten quite filthy. And the fact that she was in a place like this on a night of the full moon meant she was one of those anarchists who didn't attend the meetings.

She met my eyes and smiled mischievously.

Aah, I thought again. *I know the look in those eyes.* This particular look, like she was troubled, like she was laughing. Maybe it was a Bamboo thing.

I guess I didn't look the slightest bit afraid, so the girl approached me quietly. I really wasn't scared, though. I'd started to feel like I didn't care if I died right then and there, like nothing mattered anymore.

"What's your name?"

"Nako."

"Me, so, like, I'm Marika."

"Are we maybe around the same age?"

"I became a Bamboo when I was fifteen, and, um…so maybe sixty years ago? Huh? Maybe more? I dunno anymore!"

I slowly reached out a hand to wipe away the dirt from her face. She yanked her jaw away in surprise.

Just then, snow started to fall. We both looked up at the sky at the same time. The first snow of the year, it was desperately beautiful as it danced down. The clouds slid by, and the full moon half disappeared.

I set to work getting most of the dirt off her face. Marika stood still and narrowed her eyes happily. I was just glad I could make friends with another Bamboo like this. Because things were difficult at home. So maybe that was why—or maybe it was because I'd gotten a little weird, after all—I wasn't really bothered by the fact that there was a dead body right next to me.

"You're not going to the meeting?" I untangled her hair while I was at it.

"Huh?! You really know your stuff, huh, Nako?"

"Oh. Yeah. Um…"

"I don't go! Too annoying! But at least I know where the meeting is held!" she declared, thrusting her chest out. And then she looked at me and muttered, "Hey, maybe I could take you?" like she wanted me to like her or something. I nodded, delighted.

Marika had me climb on her back and then shot up into the night sky without any preamble whatsoever. The winter wind howled as it bit at my cheeks. I held my breath, and we cut through the night.

We raced upward through the night sky to a point half-way between the town below and the town above. And then Marika cocked her head as if to say "Huh?" and came back down. Apparently, she'd passed it.

Dropping down suddenly near a slanted factory on the road to school, she let me off behind a tree and stepped toward the building on tiptoes. The exterior walls were covered in galvanized sheet iron and pocked with holes here and there. Then she beckoned me with a hand, and I drew close too. I peered inside as instructed.

The fish cannery. The production line operated or didn't depending on the day, perhaps because of the poor economy, so even if you were lucky enough to get hired on, there were lots of days when there was no work. Yoji still brought cans home for me all the time, though.

Inside, countless candles flickered and shimmered, densely packed together. The flames were dazzling. People were also in there, standing among the candlesticks. Lots of them. Silent. Stiff, like unlit candles.

Aah! So this is the meeting!

I couldn't believe how easily I'd made it to this secret place. Lost in the moment, I looked for my Bamboo, Mustah, in his black shirt. But the plant was filled with so many people it was hard to pick him out of the crowd.

The majority of people were wearing hats in primary colors like red and blue, or massive crowns, or had silver decorations swinging on their heads. Right. On meeting nights, Yoji always left the house carrying a red hat. When I saw the Bamboo in a group like this, the hats looked like these festival costumes I'd seen somewhere a long time ago, on indigenous tribes up in the mountains in China. Which I guess meant these were ancient Bamboo who had crossed the ocean from that far-off country. Oh, and sprinkled through the crowd were also people in simple clothing, like what Mustah wore. Maybe these were the younger ones who'd become Bamboo in Japan.

I listened in and heard someone talking. The voice was that of a child. And there was something like a shining silver throne in the center?

Marika yanked on my ear roughly.

"Ow!" I was startled. "W-what?"

"We're going. They'll see us."

"Oh! So like—" She abruptly shoved me onto her back, and in the blink of an eye, we were dancing up into the night sky again. *Hyoooo!* The wind howled in my ears.

Then I remembered that if you told a human being the time or the place of the meeting, they cut off one of your arms as punishment. But when I thought about it, this stray Bamboo had just killed a living human being and drank his blood. That was a much more serious crime. She'd be locked up in a barrel and buried in the ground for that. So this Marika didn't go to meetings, and she didn't care about the rules at all?

I finally started to be a little afraid. Maybe my head had cleared. When I remembered Mustah, I felt homesick suddenly and started wanting to make it home alive again. I was angry and hurt, but I didn't actually want it to end like this, with me never seeing Mustah and Yoji again.

We flew straight ahead into the night sky. Marika was clearly used to flying since she was pretty good at it, but the ride was a bit bumpy. We began making our way back to the town below.

"So you don't worry about the rules, huh?" I asked.

Marika snorted in surprise. "Nako, you really do know your stuff, huh! But, like, it doesn't matter what I do. No, I mean, like, *I* decide what I do. I always follow my own rules."

The snowfall grew heavier. The full moon began to disappear. My breath was frozen. I was freezing. Maybe because the body of this stray Bamboo was cold as ice.

"I only eat the bad ones."

"Huh?"

"Like, guys who kill people and don't get caught! Guys

who trap people and then pretend like they had nothing to do with it! I only pick guys like that."

So you're not like God then, eh? I replied, but only in my head.

The god of this town stole lives, ripped them up from the root, and it didn't matter how good the person was or how hard they were working to move forward. None of that mattered to this god. This god did the deed like a starving beast. Was Marika's eating people any different?

We danced back down to the place we had started from. The man in the work clothes was already frozen solid. Marika kicked at his body violently and sent it flying. Her long black hair was swept up in the wind and swung around wildly, and I watched in fascination.

"This guy here, he killed somebody!"

"What?"

"I been living under the prefab school for ages. I hear all kinds of things down there. Last month, the teacher there, he got killed, you know. This is the guy who did it. For money, that's all."

My whole body shook. I peered at the body lying on its back, a block of ice on the ground. It was the old janitor guy. Mr. Yu's childhood friend, the one who used to go to school with him way back when. He had aged terribly these last few years. His frosted eyebrows had gray hairs in among the black.

God never did this for me. Retribution. Punishing the wicked.

I stood stock-still and looked down at the terrible death agony on his face.

"Can we hang out again?" Marika's voice wavered unsteadily and was yet somehow sweet.

The question brought me back to myself. I nodded slowly. It felt like the earth under my feet had tilted off to one side and a tiny me had slipped and fell into the hands of something very bad. But I wanted to see her again. I did. Before I knew it, I was peeking at her wide eyes and returning her smile.

The snowfall grew still heavier.

◆ ◆ ◆

"It's time for you to pull yourself together, Kyo! You've been totally spaced out for I don't know how many weeks, and now you're really losing it!"

"I'm not losing it. Whatever. Shut up."

"Now, look!"

The next night, I sat on the sofa, mouth half-open, absent even as they nagged and yelled. Yoji was pacing intently around me, while Mustah just watched from the side.

I hadn't gone to school again. Because I'd been up until dawn, I'd slept the whole day. And when I'd woken up in the evening, I was annoyed at the idea of sitting and waiting for the whiny Bamboo to leave for work. I wanted to go and see Marika.

Yoji had somehow realized that something was going on, but he had no idea what it was, and he was irritated. This was annoying, and I kept my eyes turned away.

"Enough! Just leave him!" Mustah said, in an unusually cold voice.

What? I felt my heart jump and shrink.

"Mustah. You say that, but it'll be too late once something actually happens. It's just, what exactly *is* the something…"

"That's why I'm telling you—just leave him!"

"Why on earth am I so worried, though? Hmm, Mustah?"

"Let's just go, Yoji!"

After they finished their nimble boxing-match grooming session, they flew off into the night sky, from where the snow that had started last night continued to fall. I saw them off out of the corner of my eye.

A complicated jumble of emotions welled up in my heart; I was relieved but also so sad I could hardly stand it. At any rate, the straightforward love I had had for them, the simple joy of just being with them, that profound happiness—it all felt like a fond memory to me now. Maybe it was because I had been a child then. Growing up, changing. That complexity.

The flames of the candles flickered fiercely in the frozen wind.

◆ ◆ ◆

Snowflakes wafted down to the icy ground. My breath was white. The ends of my fingers were cold. The tips of my long hair were almost frozen now. As I wiped at her face, Marika looked like she could hardly contain her delight. She grinned, flashing the pearly teeth in her large mouth. This grin, the look of her face—it was all very Bamboo indeed, so I was also utterly delighted.

Tonight made it a whole week of going to hang out with Marika once night fell. I'd washed her ragged clothing, done up the buttons the right way. Her hair had been tangled like a rat's nest, so I'd cut it short. I'd put lipstick on her too, a little mark of femininity for the girl Bamboo. And Marika actually cleaned up pretty well, revealing a good-looking girl beneath the mess of hair and rags. But every night, by the time we met, she would be filthy again. I got used to it soon enough and set about tidying her up, my own little boxing match. It was fun.

"But, like, okay."

"Whaaat?"

"You're the only one who gets to grin here, Nako. I mean, I can't see my own face! I haven't seen it in aaaaaages."

"But, I mean, you should show up in photos, right?"

"Liar! I did that forever ago, and it didn't work."

"Probably 'cause you used a digital camera. Bamboo totally show up on film. I don't know why, though… Right. You wanna try it?" I said, wanting her to like me.

Marika nodded gleefully, so I got even happier. She let me on her back, and we whooshed through the night sky. When I stepped into my empty house, Marika followed me, ever so timid. She still had her shoes on, though, so I hurriedly got them off of her. And of course the soles of her bare feet were filthy too, so I wiped them off with a cloth.

I pulled a Polaroid camera off the shelf and took her picture. Marika leaped back like a wild animal at the sound of the shutter, and I laughed. I dried the photo that slid out of the machine and handed it to her.

"Whoa! My face!"

"You look really cute in this, huh?"

"Okay! You too!"

"Oh! No, I do—"

Marika grabbed a different camera and pressed the shutter roughly. At an angle so that I was in it too. I snatched the machine from her hands.

"This camera, you have to take the film in to be developed. And if we do that, they'll find out."

"They? Who?"

"Oh! Umm."

"And, like, this house—whose is it?"

I tried to answer, said nothing.

"I got it!" Marika scrunched her face up spitefully, like she was suddenly burning with jealousy. "Some idiot Bamboo's keeping you here as a pet, right, Nako?"

"No! That's not it! It's…" I fell silent for a moment. And then: "They're raising me. They love me."

"…Why are you mad? You got a super-scary look on your face!"

"I'm not mad. It's just, like, I don't care what you say about me, but I don't want anyone to say anything bad about them."

When I rebuked her, Marika's face grew even stiffer for some reason. She took up the thread seriously and began to mock me. "Oooh, Nako! Bamboo pet! A big ol' dummy who'll do whatever a Bamboo says!"

"Marika!"

"Do what I tell you too!"

I was surprised by how cute her angry face was. So cute that I swooned, and my knees almost buckled beneath me. I'd never gotten the appeal of girls, but in that moment, I felt it like a flash of insight. I was seized by some power I didn't understand. My shoulders slumped, and I hung my head. "Fine. But what am I supposed to do, Marika?"

The girl gave me a triumphant grin.

◆ ◆ ◆

From that night on, surprisingly, I began to obey Marika's orders. She made me look into all kinds of things during the day. Which is why I started wearing my uniform, riding my scooter, and going to school again. That said, I didn't go to class; I just stayed in the library all day. After sunset, I'd meet up with Marika and tell her what I'd learned.

At some point, it started to feel like a dream. *Aah, if only I could be close like this with Marika forever.* I mean, *this* Bamboo needed me. So I also secretly thought that someday, perhaps in the near future, she would transform me.

Looking at it from this perspective, I really appreciated how keenly Bamboo needed partners. Since meeting me, Marika was a different person. She was clean, her face animated. The time alone must be too great a burden for grass monsters, given that they couldn't see themselves in mirrors, lived such long lives, and walked the night. Yoji had probably been like that too, back when he was all alone. He'd been reborn when he'd found the partner he had in Mustah.

But I wondered whom I'd want to be with if I managed to become a Bamboo. Would I hang out forever with my sweet Marika like this? Or would *he* become my beloved, after all? I didn't really know myself. I had only just met Marika. But I had been with Mustah since I was ten years old. He hadn't changed a bit from that night. He was still my Bamboo.

My research during the day was about crimes that happened in the town above—murders, corruption, cold cases. In both the town above and the town below, the police and the courts were ineffectual. It was rare for anyone to be arrested, no matter how terrible the crime. Meanwhile, Marika needed to eat. And also sought the thrill of the hunt. Which was why I found the criminals, and Marika flew.

High up in the winter sky, an Asian girl with short hair and red lipstick appeared, and by the time she was charging down toward your carotid artery, it was already too late. For organization men in expensive suits, getting out of foreign luxury cars. For groups of youths who attacked shops in the middle of the night and left the ancient owners dying in pools of blood. For a man who had "accidentally" knocked his stepchild into a well. Divine punishment dropped down from the sky.

God might not have been able to tell the difference between good souls and bad, but Marika could.

The extraordinary blood-soaked memory of what I had experienced that night long ago lived on in my heart. It had been there the whole time. I was loved, I had a happy life, I worked hard in school—but it was still there. It was always there. Holding its breath, hiding. Which was why this little game of "stealing flames" was so cruelly enjoyable.

One night, we were walking along together when we heard a scream. Instantly, Marika got excited and flew off. I chased after her to find a woman on the ground. A prostitute, still young, slender, elegant. Her makeup was on the thick side, but I could tell she was around the same age as me. She had been knocked unconscious. The ass of the man hunched over her was swarthy, shining. The snow danced down around him, and his skin glistened wetly.

Marika was pleased. She dropped down in a straight line. The man looked over his shoulder.

"Ah! Marika!" There was a strange edge to my voice.

"What?!" Marika stopped and floated in the sky, turning baffled eyes on me. "Stay out of my way!"

"Let him go. Please… He's a friend."

"Hey, is that maybe Professor Nako?" Niita called to me quietly. His pants down around his ankles, he stared at me, looking foolish, naked from the waist down. His knees were on the ground, which was wet from the snow.

"Huh? Your friend? This sick pervert?" The look on Marika's face said she was having none of it. And she wanted blood. She bared her teeth ferociously. I probably wouldn't be able to stop her again.

I screwed up my face and shouted, "Niita! Run!"

"Huh?"

"You know criminals are being hunted down and killed lately, right? It's all been me and this girl! So listen, just run! Go! Hurry!"

"You and your friend? Killing criminals? Huh? But what happened to high school?"

"I'm telling you, go! Don't look back, just run! Don't ever let me see your face again—" My throat choked shut.

In my ears, I suddenly heard Niita's clear voice from that day long ago.

Nako! he called, in a voice filled with affection. *If you grow up and turn into garbage, then there'll be nothing for me to believe in in this town.*

I dropped to my knees on the spot and buried my face in

my hands. I thought of the time that had passed. Grieved for the things I'd loved.

The snow sparkled and scattered, fluttering down in the sky. A faint wind blew. I heard footsteps, Niita running away with my past. The snowflakes were beautiful again tonight.

♦ ♦ ♦

Niita had changed. And so had I. Now I was partner to a stray Bamboo who hunted people at night. I had also become someone who stole flames.

♦ ♦ ♦

For a few days after that, I stayed home, even after night fell. I kept my head down when Marika came flying around outside the window. She might have been a stray Bamboo, but even she hesitated to actually come all the way into the house. After a while, she'd give up and fly off somewhere. But she'd be back again the next night, sitting still in the darkness, like a dog waiting for its master.

I opened up my textbooks, thinking I might start going to class again, though it was fairly late for that. But it would be winter break soon, and if I worked really hard, I could probably catch up—that's what I thought. I wondered if it would work.

And then, at the start of that night, that fateful night, Mustah, supposedly gone off to work, came flying back. Yoji was close behind him, seemingly in a panic, and grabbed hold of Mustah's arm as if to try to stop him.

What's all this? I looked up from my textbook.

The look on Mustah's face was one of absolute fury. I'd never seen him so angry. I figured for sure he'd found out I hadn't been going to class, and a shiver ran through me.

"Kyo!" His voice was fierce. "Who is this?!" He shoved a photograph at me.

I gasped. It was a picture of me and Marika. From that time when she'd come inside and mistakenly pressed the shutter. I'd carelessly left the film in the camera.

"Um…" I looked up fearfully. "My new friend."

"Is she human? No! She's Bamboo, isn't she?"

"Um…"

"And I've never seen her face at the meetings. A stray Bamboo, huh? And that's this room behind you, isn't it? You didn't actually let her in here?!"

"Mustah—"

"What have you been doing at night with a stray Bamboo?!"

"But she's…not…a bad kid," I started to say, and then closed my mouth. Because the truth was I knew only too well that Marika was a bad kid. That she wasn't like Mustah and Yoji, that she was a dangerous anarchist monster. And now I was doing things I totally could never tell them about. Playing at stealing the flames of other humans…

Mustah flipped the table over violently and then moved on to overturning all kinds of other things. All I could do was stagger fearfully along behind him like an idiot. I heard Yoji's chiding voice, but it seemed like Mustah didn't.

"Um, okay, it's 'cause, like, I can't be close with you and Yoji anymore."

"Huh?" He whirled his terrible face around.

"I was lonely. And then I met this Bamboo, and she was sincerely, for real, happy to be with me…"

"We can't be close? What are you even talking about?! We're the same as always. We've just been fighting a bit lately."

"But you're going to go off and leave me…"

"You're totally wrong. We're not going to run off and leave you. *You're* going to grow up and be an amazing person someday. Seriously, Kyo, you gotta get it together!"

"I just thought…like, maybe, if we were friends, she might make me a Bamboo…"

Mustah suddenly fell silent. He narrowed his eyes sharply and stared at me. This was much scarier than the outburst before. I trembled violently and nervously looked down at him. His shoulders slumped heavily.

"What the hell…"

"But, I mean, I—"

"I should never have taken in a kid like you! I should've left you where I found you! It would have been better if those men had shot you!"

"Mustah! Take that back!" I shouted.

I tried to grab at him, and Yoji flew between us to stop me. He turned not toward me, but toward Mustah. "That is not okay! Talking so violently like that! Right, Kyo, hon? You'll just scare the poor boy."

"But, I mean—no matter what we say, he just doesn't get it! Is he an idiot?!"

"Mustah! Come on. Maybe he didn't turn out exactly how we wanted, but you can't blame Kyo for that."

"Huh?"

"The flame is free. That's exactly why it's a flame."

"Unh. Well…"

"But when he's courting danger, we have to sit him down and tell him that. We have to discuss it," Yoji insisted, quietly.

Mustah slowly nodded and sat down on the sofa. He was about to say something, but then he spat, "I can't! My blood's all gone to my head!"

So it was Yoji who sat me down on the sofa next to him and started telling me about how dangerous a stray Bamboo could be. I sat quietly and listened. Mustah went out onto the terrace, turned his back to me, and sat on the bench.

When Yoji was done talking, I knew things I hadn't before. I promised I wouldn't see Marika anymore. The Bamboo flew off into the night sky once more. Yoji looked back and nodded gently, as if to say it was okay. Mustah didn't look at me at all. I hung my head and pulled my knees to my chest.

◆ ◆ ◆

I left the house and began walking down the night road. Almost as if she'd been waiting impatiently for me, Marika swooped down in great delight, causing gusts of wind to spring up around me. Her playful grin really did resemble Mustah's look of deep affection, a face I didn't get to see very often these days. And to be honest, I didn't want to let this smiling face go. But…

I had very clearly promised Yoji, so in a small voice, I announced, "Sorry, I can't see you like this anymore, Marika."

Marika was dumfounded. Her lips trembled. "Got it!" she barked, sounding angry. "Your master told you not to, huh!"

"No. And he's not my master. If I had to say, he's my papa. My fifth papa."

"Fifth?"

"Yeah. The first four were human, though. My Bamboo papa's the nicest of them all."

"Weird! But we were having so much fun together every night!"

"Hey, Marika?" I grew worried. In a small voice, I said, "So, like, go find a proper Bamboo partner, instead of human like me. And start going to the meetings, okay?"

The instant I gave voice to this, I realized that, at some point, I had stopped wanting so desperately to be made into a Bamboo. The things my beloved papas had told me over and over and over again—I had taken the long way round and was starting, bit by bit, to accept the idea of growing up, stoking the fire and becoming an adult, and finally, of getting old.

Marika twisted up her face. "I'm not going to any meetings!" she yelled. "They'll arrest me!"

"Oh, right. The punishment's sixty years buried in a barrel, right?" I smiled.

"Yeah. Well! I only kill the bad ones, so maybe they'll take that into consideration and make it shorter. And, like, if they catch me now, there's that thing in fifteen years."

"That thing?"

"The dude sitting on the throne at the meeting, all full of himself? Name's Ruirui, one of the royal family from China, 'kay? Still, he's nothing more than the shabby king of the Bamboo in this town now, maybe two hundred of 'em at best. There's this thing, like a festival, celebrating fifty years since his enthronement. So maybe the prisoners in barrels'll be given amnesty."

"You sure know a lot about it, Marika."

A fair bit of snow had piled up on either side of the road. I slipped and nearly fell, and Marika reached out a hand to hold me up. I laughed to myself. Humans are so weird. On a snowy road like this we should just fly, and yet we can't do that.

The sky was pitch-black. The falling snowflakes shone individually, reflecting the little light there was.

Ah, it's so beautiful. And you know, it had been a long time since I'd really looked at the sky. This was maybe the first time since the night of the big fight. I felt like I was finally waking up from a bad dream.

The world during the day was actually beautiful. The way the ocean glittered in the morning. The giant columns of clouds that spread out in the summer sky. The radiant green leaves. The heat of the sand on the soles of your feet. The fragrant scent when the sweat that came along with that heat dried instantly in the sunlight.

The Bamboo couldn't experience this daytime world. They didn't grow, either. So they didn't get the fond feeling that this brilliance was only for the present moment. The conviction that I wanted to be a Bamboo started to fade soundlessly from my heart.

"Bamboo life's kinda weird," I said, jokingly.

Marika grinned, playfully. And then her face got serious. "So, like, Nako?"

"Yeah."

"This has been kinda bugging me. But this is goodbye, so I guess I'll just ask you. Are you, like, a boy?"

"What?!" I panicked.

Which made Marika flustered too. "No!" she continued, hurriedly. "I mean, it's no big deal. It's just, you smell different from girls! It started to bug me, you know? But why are you pretending to be a girl? And since when?"

"That's—ever since I was ten. People are after me, you know? My Bamboo are worried about me, so they made me dress like this. Said I'd be killed if anyone found out I was a boy."

Marika suddenly got a serious look on her face and nodded. "So that's it. Okay, I'll keep it to myself. I won't tell a soul. You can relax."

"Yeah."

"Hey, but…are we really not going to hang out anymore?" Her voice was sad. Her eyes seemed soft. She was actually incredibly cute. I could hardly stand it.

I went to answer her but stopped abruptly. "Huh? Marika, did you hear something? From above?"

The next moment, something, not snow, shone in the night sky… Several silhouettes dropped down, lustrous capes fluttering.

"Huh?" Before we knew it, we were completely surrounded. Me and Marika.

Adult men and women. More than ten of them. Most were Asian or Central or South American, but there were also two white Russians. From the way they held themselves, they were definitely not amateurs. They were different from even the guys on the bottom rung of the organization in the town above. There was no wasted movement. They were eerily expressionless.

And they had come flying down from the sky. I thought, *They're Bamboo!*

Yoji's voice came back to me: *First of all, people are after her. You can't run from them.*

Marika grabbed my wrist and tried to leap into the sky, but she was slapped down like a mosquito and fell to the ground. She hit the snow hard. My arms were twisted back, and I was pushed down face-first.

From above us, I heard a low voice. "Secured!"

♦ ♦ ♦

"Two offenders."

The open but nonoperational cannery. Past midnight. Candlesticks were set out, and candles in a variety of designs hurriedly lit. Then, in what had looked like a vast, empty darkness, I saw face after pale face emerge into the shallow light. They had been there in the darkness. They had been there the whole time. People in garish primary-colored hats and head dressings. The Bamboo who walked the night.

No one said anything; they simply glared in my direction, looking angry. They looked like Mustah when he was in a bad mood. *Aah, there really is a Bamboo look,* I thought.

In the center of the immense space was the ancient silver throne. Sitting there was a child of twelve or thirteen from the looks of him, a heavy, shiny blue thing on his head that swung each time he moved. At least, he was probably a boy. The pitch of his voice, untouched by puberty, was innocent, in total dissonance with the fierceness of the edge in it. He held a sheet of orange paper in his hand, and this he spread out importantly.

I was in the center of this apparently hastily convened meeting, made to sit on my knees on the ground. One of my wrists was bound by handcuffs, locked to a post driven into the dirt floor.

"Now, now, the first one." The boy raised his hand ponderously, accompanied by the rustling of fabric, and the Bamboo let their eyes roam.

The boy was probably the one Marika had told me about— Ruirui, the son of the royal family who had come from the depths of China on an immigrant ship. He looked like he had just started junior high school, but I was sure he was actually a super-old man. There was an indescribable coldness in the depths of his eyes. Just like with the other Bamboo, I couldn't read the look on his face. Not anger, not contempt, nothing. His eyes frightened me to the core; they made me feel like I would be sucked into their pitch-black centers at any moment, trapped in the oxygenless depths of outer space.

On his signal, Marika was dragged out and roughly tossed before him.

"Ah!" I cried out, because I could see at a glance she'd been tortured. Her left arm had been torn off—it was completely gone—and one of her ears was missing. When I looked carefully, I saw that the tip of her nose had also been shaved away. She was half-naked. Her head lolled to one side, her whole body limp. She didn't meet my eyes.

"Marika…" Had her arm been ripped off because she'd told me, a human, where the meeting was? Had they found out? I was the one who'd made her tell me, though. She'd just been trying to make this human happy.

And then a middle-aged man stepped up to the throne, elegant, with perfect posture, and handed the boy a paper to read. "Name: Marika," he announced, in a plain-spoken voice. "Age: estimated to be around seventy. Gender: female. And her crimes are two. First, the crime of bringing a human to the meeting place and allowing the human to see, half in jest."

A murmur rose up. All at once, all Bamboo eyes were on me. I shrank back.

Suddenly, I wondered if my Bamboo were among the crowd. I lifted my face and quickly looked around. But all I could see were pale faces and hats and feet lit up here and there in the thick darkness, so I couldn't really tell.

"And the crime of killing and eating humans. At least seven confirmed."

Ruirui continued. "Thus, our judgment is—"

"W-wait!" I shouted desperately, to stop Ruirui from continuing his stilted speech in his high voice, like he was reading from the orange paper.

"Eh?" His voice could not have been colder. With his gaze, he looked at me as though he were peering down at a stray dog on the side of the road.

When I met those eyes, I shivered again. Such cold, empty eyes. But I mustered up my courage. I mean, Marika had said, after all, that they might take that extra stuff into consideration and give her a shorter sentence. And she was in such pain she couldn't speak anymore. I had to...

"It's true that Marika did kill people. But..." The Bamboo stirred once again. "She only targeted criminals, liars, and cheats. People who hadn't been caught for doing bad things. I know it was still wrong and against the law. But, please... have even just a little mercy on her."

"We have investigated." Ruirui's tone was unchanged, still icy. He gave a signal to the older man next to him.

The man explained, "With the cooperation of a human accomplice, Marika found and attacked criminals. The accomplice's investigative skills were indeed solid, and I think quite sharp for a high school student. Unfortunately, the human she killed before the accomplice appeared was falsely accused."

"…Falsely accused?"

"A school teacher was assaulted and killed by a thief. Marika attacked the man she assumed to be the criminal. A janitor from the same workplace."

The image of Marika crouched over him, drinking his blood the night we first met, came back to my mind. So it was that time…

"But he was not the perpetrator."

"No way…"

"The locals have an inkling of this as well, but it seems they didn't go out of their way to report it. The criminal is rumored to be a man who was once his student. Someone who lives in poverty and has committed repeated acts of violence on the road at night. Apparently, in this case, he didn't realize that his target was someone he knew. His name is Niita."

Niita? I stared up at the man, dumbfounded.

He stared down at me. "The residents started to say this a few days after the incident. No one told you, hmm?"

Ashamed, I slowly shook my head. I mean, I hadn't seen anyone. The more I chased my dreams, the further away I got from my old friends.

The wind blew in through the open doors, bringing gusts of snow with it. The flames of the candles flickered.

I hung my head.

"Thus it is deemed that there are no extenuating circumstances to consider in this crime," Ruirui continued in his high voice. "Marika shall be imprisoned for sixty years! Given her presumed age of approximately seventy, she will likely reach the end of her life in the earth, burst into bloom alone, and disappear. Hmph! It's quite the fitting punishment. Ready the barrel!"

An elliptical-looking barrel came rolling out from somewhere noisily, and they threw Marika in roughly, like she was a thing. Then a heavy machine roared into the factory and started digging a hole in the earth. Dirt came flying in my direction. A lid was placed on the barrel, and then the whole thing was dropped into the hole. Marika's anguished screams filled the vast space.

I wanted to plug my ears. My knees shook in fear. Earth was tossed onto the barrel in the hole until I could no longer see the top of it. Marika's voice gradually grew fainter until it faded from my ears.

Silence fell. There was only the sound of the blowing wind now. The candles flickered gently.

"Now, then." His voice fearsome, Ruirui turned toward me. As if to say, this is where the real party starts.

I trembled, but I didn't avert my eyes.

"A problem! There is a grave problem! According to Marika's testimony, this human has extremely detailed knowledge about the life of the Bamboo, yes? Ladies and gentlemen, can this be tolerated? It means that someone has taught this human about us. Someone among the Bamboo gathered together here tonight! From what we've heard, this human was somehow lovingly raised by Bamboo instead of receiving the love of a parent, yes?!" Ruirui shouted all in one breath.

I didn't know how he'd managed his declaration without a moment to inhale. That was scary too, and I was frozen in place, all the courage drained out of me. The chain attached to my wrist shook every so often. The uncomfortable clamoring of the Bamboo grew louder.

"It did take some time to get all this out of her, however. Fwoh! Fwoh! Fwoh! Gyah! Gyah!" Ruirui had a strange way of laughing. His appearance and voice were those of a child, but the way he wrinkled up his face and curled into himself as he guffawed was all old man.

I remembered Marika's shaved nose, her missing ear. A Bamboo's injuries closed over soon enough, but anything cut off wouldn't grow back. She had been tortured because she'd become friends with me. I bit my lip. What was I going to do? Marika!

"This girl…"

Huh?

Ruirui stretched out a plump, childish hand and pointed at me, and I realized that Marika hadn't told them I was actually a boy, in hiding because the organization in the town above was after my life. Even after being tortured like that, she hadn't given them a single extra thing.

So that's it. Okay, I'll keep it to myself. I won't tell a soul. You can relax. Marika's animated voice filled my ears, and I held back my tears.

"Who, I wonder," Ruirui continued, "is this master Marika spoke of?"

Someone came up from behind me and twisted my arm in the opposite direction. I cried out in pain.

"All we know is the address. A small cottage by the beach. Now, there aren't too many Bamboo living in that area. Because we are descended from a mountain people and do not care for the sea, hmm? So it would seem we have a some-what eccentric Bamboo on our hands. We were, however, not able to get a name from the criminal, unfortunately. Now then, let us see…"

The cavernous space was utterly silent. My own cries were the only interruption.

Finally, they dragged people out of the herd of Bam-boo. One from deep on the right. And one more from the opposite side. A man with dark skin and a beard in a black shirt—Mustah. A red hat in the folk tradition and a white shirt—Yoji. Both were expressionless, like waxwork. They were trying not to look at me. I too desperately tried to avert my eyes. My arm was wrenched again, and I screamed. Yoji twitched and looked back reflexively. I twisted my neck and tried to get them out of my field of view.

"About the only ones who live in that area are these two, hmm? Gyah gyah gyah!"

"I don't know. Either. I've. Never seen. These people! Ah!" My arm was jerked back so fiercely I thought it would be ripped off.

"It's obviously one of them!" Ruirui continued in his high voice. With a look in his eyes that said he wouldn't let us get away. "Or should we burn both?"

Burn? Execution by fire?

I gasped.

Noticing that the color had drained from my face, Ruirui flashed me a curious smile. "Now then, who raised you?"

My mouth was dry. Outside, a bird sang. The sky had been pitch-black, but now a faint light was starting to grow in the direction of the ocean. The flames of the candles flickered and snapped in the wind. The snow was ice-cold.

"It's getting to be dawn. We're out of time. Aah, such a bother. It'd just be easier to punish them both, hmm?"

"Stop. Please stop." I shook my head. And I looked at Mustah and Yoji, my face still turned to the ground.

They both had someone behind them twisting their arms and pushing them forward. I couldn't read either of their faces. They weren't signaling me in any way, either, not trying to tell me, *Kyo, do this, Kyo, do that*. Yoji with his pale skin, his quiet eyes. Mustah's entire body was stiff either in anger or in fear.

I remembered that I'd fought with Mustah before and we still hadn't made up. Lately, it was always like that. It had been better when I was a kid. I hated this. I couldn't stand it.

"Now then, now then." Ruirui's voice echoed through the great hall. It was almost like he was speaking right next to my ear. A hypnotic echo.

I inhaled sharply. The snowy wind blew in from outside, threatening to extinguish the flames of the candles. The color of the sky gradually changed.

"Which one were you raised by, Nako, or whatever you're called?"

"Stop... Don't ask me..."

"Then they'll both die. Is that what you want?"

"No! No!"

Mustah. My Bamboo. Please! Don't die!

I reached out a trembling hand and pointed squarely at the Bamboo in the white shirt.

In that instant, I knew it. I was still only seventeen years old, but this was the greatest sin of my life, the one I'd never be able to atone for. Even so, I couldn't not commit this sin.

I was basically the same as the shitheel god of this town! Someone who happily destroyed good people without any distinction between the good or evil of their souls.

Or... It suddenly hit me.

Maybe God had never been happy about any of this.

Maybe.

I didn't know anything. I was so very foolish.

Day started to break, and the Bamboo disappeared one by one from the cannery. The flames of the candles were also extinguished and the candlesticks put away. A stake was hammered into the ground near the entrance, and they chained Yoji to it. And not just one hand like me; they wound the chain tightly around both hands, both feet, his neck, and his torso.

"Now, then!" Finally, I heard Ruirui's voice echoing throughout the now nearly empty cannery. He too was making to leave, receding step-by-step to somewhere. "Yoji shall be burned at the stake. For the crime of taking in a human child, raising it, and teaching it details about the Bamboo. This is a very serious crime. Gyah!"

Mustah had vanished at some point. Ruirui's laughter also departed up into the night sky, while I sat stunned on the ground.

Yoji had only just talked with me at the house. Calmly but clearly, he had carefully explained to me the reasons why I couldn't spend time with a stray Bamboo. In the end, I had agreed, and we had nodded at each other in understanding. Even though he had had such a small amount of time left in this life of raising me, of courting this danger.

"Accept everything," Yoji said, mysteriously. And then he cocked his head to one side and stared at me.

Yoji! That face! I would never forget it as long as I lived.

Finally, all of the Bamboo were gone from the plant, leaving only Yoji and me, chained up. The sun slowly rose in the eastern sky, and the weak light of winter shone in through the open doors. A cold white fog—no, smoke started to rise up from Yoji's body. I let out a long scream.

He looked straight up at the sun. Eyes narrowed at the brilliance of it. His body was still, like he was praying. It wasn't fear.

But the moment I understood that it was all over—that face in profile! What can I say?

As I watched his pale skin burn black, my face crumpled. His body also writhed and burned, smoking. He was ostensibly being burned at the stake, but there were hardly any flames. Yoji gradually grew smaller, charred. There was the smell of charcoal, and then finally he shook slightly. And vanished.

◆ ◆ ◆

Yoji had been around for a long time. Since long before I had been born. He had seen history. He was the kind of person who reread a book of poetry he'd brought over from China and wept. Gentle, lyrical, and wholehearted in raising the human child he had taken in for just over seven years.

What does it mean to be alive? I asked myself. The answer was, of course, the same.

That your heart moves. Love someone, find something beautiful, seek growth, be incredibly ashamed of yourself. And feel strongly.

This Bamboo's kind heart had moved like that in life. And yet.

All the good people went too soon. The boss had taken my sister. Niita, Mr. Yu. Me, Yoji. We had made them die!

The peaceful sky somewhere off in the distance was over-crowded with the souls of good people.

Staring at the charred ground, nothing but the stake and chains remaining, I sent my heart off into space. I fled into my memories of sweet, pleasurable days.

Eventually, the sun grew high in the sky, and I could hear the voices of children playing from afar. But I couldn't bring myself to cry out "Someone!" for help. My head still hanging, noon came, and then the day fell back into shadow bit by bit.

And then, around the time the dusk shone red, announcing the arrival of night, the sound of footfalls came from a distance. When I lifted my head, I saw a human silhouette racing into the plant. I strained my eyes.

It was a man covered head to toe in black fabric. Something like the curtain for a darkroom. His face was hidden beneath it; I couldn't see a bit of it. He held a large ax in his right hand. He looked like the god of death himself. But I wouldn't flee anymore. I simply stared up at him.

There was a voice. "Kyo!"

The brandished ax shot into the air. The blade glittered sharply.

"I'm here!" Mustah's voice.

The ax was brought down heavily. With a dry sound, the chain binding me to the stake was cut. I felt a yank on my arm, and then I was inside the thick, black fabric. Before I knew it, arms were wrapped tightly around me. The scent of bamboo filled my nostrils.

You came to save me? But it's so dangerous still. The sun's not down yet. Yet you worry about someone like me? How deep does your kindness go exactly?

Mustah...

I tried to say I was sorry, but the words wouldn't come out. Even so, I forced my voice out to apologize finally, trembling.

"Kyo." Mustah's low voice came in my ear. "Look."

"I'm sorry, Mustah. I'm so sorry. Yoji... I...I..."

"You, okay, you stayed with a couple of guys like us."

"Mustah."

"And don't go saying you didn't have anywhere else to go!"

"Uh-huh..."

"Come on. Don't hurt like this, Kyo. Forget it already. Everything about this night. This had to be our fate, the three of us. The good stuff, the bad stuff, all of it... This kind of thing's in that book of Chinese poetry Yoji liked. Although I can't actually read it. A long time ago, he told me. On a night when we sat next to each other on the bench and talked."

I wiped my tears away and looked at Mustah. Under the black fabric, I couldn't really see his face. I couldn't tell if he was grinning foolishly or was morose and sullen.

He helped wipe my tears away with the back of his hand, clumsily. I held my breath inside the fabric.

"Mustah…"

I heard a noise and saw a different blade had appeared in his hand at some point. Scissors. He cut off the hair that hung down to my waist. My head shorn, I covered it with both hands.

"Change your clothes." He handed me Yoji's shirt and jeans.

Why? I asked with my eyes inside the black fabric.

"You're not safe anymore. I mean, you know too much about the Bamboo. They won't kill you, y'know, but they'll probably lock you up somewhere and keep you there until you die."

"Then…"

Mustah's eyes glittered under the fabric. I stared back at him, clutching the clothing to my chest. The answer came back to me.

"So! You have to run!" And we flew.

Given that he had fabric over his head and was holding me on top of that, Mustah's flying was much more erratic than usual. He spun round and round, descending abruptly until we were scraping along the ground before pulling back up again. Still, we somehow managed to finally make it to the small train station in the town above.

The sun sank down into the horizon. Mustah threw the fabric aside and finally revealed his face to me. I was relieved to see his usual smile. Or maybe he was just trying to put me at ease.

We slipped through the gates of the station and ran into the building together. Now that night had fallen, people would be coming to find me once they realized I'd escaped the cannery. Mustah found a train heading toward a distant town, the next one to depart from the station, and he thrust me onto the platform, practically flying even now.

"Kyo, this one!"

I leaped aboard the train in a trance, and then something was shoved at me from behind. Something cold. I took it wordlessly. "Little Kyo's Piggy Bank." With all the money I had made at my part-time job.

I didn't have time now to think through all the different things going on. I had to live. Fight. I had to run.

But...Mustah! *Wait, my Bamboo!*

"I won't see you again?!" I shouted, and everything felt wrong somehow. I mean, I was back to looking like a boy now. For the first time in seven years. Once my long hair was cut, my cute scarf removed, my skirt tossed aside, I was instantly the very picture of a seventeen-year-old boy. My thin, girlish voice was strange now. My words floated off into space, blown away by the winter wind. I felt like they might even shatter like actual ice.

But still. I did actually adore my Bamboo the way a girl my age would.

"Is this the end? For us?"

"It's not gonna be the end or anything, Kyo!"

"Mustah..."

"I mean, the end of us is your real beginning, y'know!"

"Mustah!" I shouted, resisting. *No, not that. I knew it. I don't want this. To forget, how awful, no. Mustah...*

More and more people crowded onto the platform. Mustah quickly looked around in a panic, fearful of the possible pursuers among them, thinking that they might have already found us. And then he peered at my face.

I was crying again. I sounded pathetic. "I'll never see you again? That can't be, Mustah. My—Mustah! I mean, Yoji's gone now too. If I go away too, like..."

"What, you worried about me? Hey, come on, I'll be fine!"

"That's—" I hiccupped. "But who's going to comb your hair all nice and neat every night? Who's going to straighten the collar of your shirt for you? You're not actually going to live with another Bamboo? Not with me, not with Yoji? That's..."

The house where the three of us had lived popped up in the back of my mind. The house I had left last night like always, not expecting that I'd never be able to go home to it again. That beloved house filled with memories. A new Bamboo, a stranger to me, would come and go, sit next to Mustah on the bench, and then together... Rage suddenly started to burn coldly in my chest.

Mustah shook his head. "He was the only partner for me."

These words, spoken with such conviction, now slowly wounded me for some reason. "H-he was..."

"So, from now on, well, I'll just go it alone."

"Alone?"

"Stop crying, Kyo. As of tonight, you're a boy again. No, as of a long time ago—the truth is, you were always a wonderful boy."

"Mustah!"

The time for the train to depart was approaching. Crowds of people walked along the platform. People jumping onto the train in a panic, buying things at kiosks. I still had things I wanted to say, but I could no longer speak. And then the doors rattled shut, and we were separated by glass.

In a panic, I ran along inside the carriage and yanked

open a window. Mustah also ran down the platform, drawing closer.

"Mustah!" I could only say his name, my heart filled with love.

He put a hand to my chest. *Huh? What's he doing?*

"Don't forget, Kyo!"

"What? What? Mustah!"

His eyes were terribly quiet. I held my breath. A powerfully gentle light shone on his face as though the late Yoji had possessed him. Like Yoji was there too, guiding me somehow.

"You have a flame here. You've always had it, from the moment you were born. That's why we protected you so desperately. You are fire. Until their very last day, until their lives are exhausted, humans are fire."

"Mustah…"

"Humans are fire!" The train started moving with a klank. "Don't forget!"

Mustah ran along the platform, chasing the train. I heard the voice of that other Bamboo, the one who was gone now, gently overlaid on Mustah's.

"As long as you always remember that, you can live through anything, no matter what kind of hard times life has in store for you. Fire! We loved that bright, special flame so deeply it practically made us crazy! No one else in this world could ever take your place. Each and every human being is a special fire! So don't go out. Live. Please, promise me you'll try. Say you'll fight. An eternal promise between the flame in your chest and your Bamboo, a promise that can never, ever be broken!"

"Mustah!" I bobbed my head up and down. "I promise. I promise. My Bamboo. My fire for you."

I promise to live. So you don't have to worry about me any-more. Don't fret over me. Don't hurt for me. I'm okay now. I know I'll get stronger. Tomorrow I'll be a different me. And the day after that, yet a different me. So…

I stretched my arm out as far as I could and gripped my Bamboo's hand. His dark skin. The palm of his hand, cold like ice. My own hand was horribly hot, like it might melt my Bamboo's.

I wanted to say, *I love you*. I wanted to become docile like a small child again and just tell him how I felt. I wanted to be straightforward. But I couldn't say it. I had already gotten too big for that.

So instead of words of love, I simply said his name over and over.

Rocking back and forth, the train picked up speed. And then…

Mustah.

Mustah.

The train pulled away from the platform. I stuck my head out the window and strained my eyes and watched as the sil-houette of my Bamboo standing stock-still on the end of the platform, seeing me off, grew more and more distant.

The train hurtled forward. Time, too, passed instanta-neously, a train itself running along a different set of rails.

GIRL

Fifteen years passed. I managed to live undiscovered and uncaptured by the Bamboo administration of that dis-tant town.

When I thought about it, they had cast a fairly tight net around that place with their power, but perhaps it was something like a spiderweb, a barrier stretching out in the sky above the town. If a human being ran far enough away, their power suddenly couldn't reach you. Plus, they would have been looking for a girl.

That night, on the train, I ran from them, with nowhere in particular to run to. And then I got off in a town far, far away. Completely unlike the town where I was born and raised, it was an easygoing, peaceful place, with none of those tribal organizations of my home. And without the gangs, the economy of this town was quietly stable, so there was no great difference between the haves and have-nots.

I didn't have parents or an academic record. Even if I'd still burned with it, the ambition I'd had to go on to higher education, to move up in the world, to become rich—almost like a desire for revenge against fate—was impossible for me to realize now. But like a fever being cured, that desire had completely vanished from within me.

Other things were more important to me now. Living in peace. Finding people to love, loving them. Being grateful.

I worked part-time at a cake shop, helping customers. Eventually, I was allowed to watch the bakers and learn their jobs so that I could help out, but only when there weren't enough people around to get the job done. My hands were nimble, and I was a quick learner, so soon I was working in both the front and the back of the shop. Three years into it, the owner said she'd make me a regular salaried employee. That said, I was a contract employee, and that contract had to be renewed every year.

Sometimes, I'd remember the time I worked at the cake

shop back when I was going to that academic school. It would suddenly hit me that I'd worked as a girl then, and it felt strange. Almost like it hadn't actually been me.

Shortcake, chocolate cake, fruit mousse, cookies—I learned how to make them all with my eyes closed. Some evenings, my older colleagues would take me out to drink. I started spending time with girls too, although I never had anything like the dazzling radiance of a first love. Maybe because I was used to girls, having been one. The fact that my first love had actually been a Bamboo and a murderer started to fade from my mind.

In my midtwenties, at the invitation of a man I'd gotten to know at a bar, I joined an amateur theater group as a hobby. I was tall, if nothing else, and there were few male actors, so I was a priceless treasure. I got a fair number of speaking roles. And some people came specifically to see me, so that was fun. It tickled me to hear my own name shouted out from the audience. *Aah, I'm alive*, I'd think. I wasn't going by my real name, Kyo, though, or my sister's name, Nako. I was using yet another, different, name.

And so the days passed like this. I came to cherish the people I met in this new town. When I thought that I might suddenly never see them or the town again, all of it felt unbearably precious to me.

I had friends too, and sometimes lovers. The theater troupe disbanded after I turned thirty. That night was like the end of a festival. At the closing party, we all slapped each other's shoulders, telling each other, "Aah, we were so young, eh?"

Eventually, the cake shop, which was in a residential area, opened up a small branch in front of the station, and it was decided that I would work there. I thought about maybe moving closer to my new workplace. Closer to the station, the rent was higher, but I could get a smaller place to offset that, and at any rate it was just me living by myself. I talked it over with my lover, and she was really put out for some reason. "Hey, whoa," she chided me. Like, wasn't it about time I settled down, wasn't I getting to be a little old for this?

Maybe it was inevitable, but, well, I did love her, and before I knew it, she was about to be put onto my family register. I couldn't help feeling that she'd played me a bit like the proverbial fiddle, though. Well, whatever. In any case, it had been fifteen years. You grow up. I worked hard, and I laughed every day.

It was a hot summer day that year, a day the news said was the hottest of the year. That night, to celebrate our engagement, a friend had planned a simple party for me and my fiancée. I closed the shop and cleaned up, and then I checked the clock and flew out the door.

There was a girl standing at the bus stop in front of the station, looking extremely troubled. She seemed like she wasn't from around here. Her clothing was somehow different. And when I saw her looking up at the bus schedules, then peering at a map, I figured she was lost.

She was wearing a large white medical mask, the kind you wear when you have a cold or it's allergy season. Her long hair wasn't done; it fluttered in the wind, a black curtain. Her physique was small, and she was thin to the point of being skinny. Well, she was like a lot of teenage girls. She wasn't incredibly attractive, but she wasn't bad either. Uninterested and in a hurry, I passed by her.

"Uh, um." The girl looked up at me.

"Hmm? Me?" With no other choice, I brought my feet to a halt, and the map was thrust at me. I was surprised. No greeting, no "excuse me," no "could you tell me," no "please" or "thank you." It was clear she wanted to ask the way, but still, the kids these days honestly had no manners. Exasperated, I begrudgingly took the map.

"Where are you trying to go? You can give me the map, but I still don't know what you want." I was also in a hurry, so my reply was curt. But I couldn't just walk away from a child in trouble. The whole situation was annoying.

The girl stared at me like she was horribly disappointed. I looked back at her, my face blank. Finally, she pointed vaguely at some spot on the map. She was so sullen it was almost rude. I realized her pale finger was shaking, and an odd feeling sprang up in me.

"What? Here? That's close. Don't get on at this stop. You'll want to get on the number five over there, okay? Get off at the seventh stop, and it'll be on the other side of the road. But, listen, what business does a kid have in a place like that? It's a temple, you know?"

"Huh? A temple?"

"Hey now, you. You pointed to this spot yourself, didn't you?"

"I know!"

"Huh?"

"I know already!" She sounded even more obstinate. But at the end of her declaration, she shuddered, like she was about to burst into tears.

Bewildered, I looked at her again. Maybe I knew her? But

the outline of her face covered by the mask and the two eyes didn't look familiar.

"Thanks, Nako. Okay, bye!"

I blinked.

"Take care, 'kay?"

In that instant, I felt a cold wind blowing at my feet, mixed with snow, knocking me back to the other side of the distant past.

Beautiful tears like pearls welled up in the girl's eyes. One dropped onto the mask and wet it. Her hair was long, and it covered her ears, so I couldn't tell if both ears were there or not. Unconsciously, I shifted my gaze to the arm opposite the one that had thrust the map out at me. The long-sleeved shirt flapped in the wind. She was missing an arm.

But…I couldn't remember her name!

Then the bus arrived, and passengers came trudging out of it. The sidewalk in front of the station was suddenly full of people. The girl turned on her heel and started walking away quickly, as if to flee.

What was your name…?

I stood there rooted to the spot for a while and then hurriedly moved to go after her. My first love—she had come all the way from the distant past, that winter's day fifteen years ago, to see me.

Just like she had been then, she was young. No, childish. And like always, she was straightforward. Right—she had protected me, hadn't she? Even though they had tortured her so horribly. She probably still hadn't told them I was actually a boy, that they'd never find a girl no matter how hard they looked. We had loved each other that much…

What was your name?

I seriously couldn't remember. Memories of how close we had been surged back into my heart, a mysterious surf. But I couldn't remember her name. I…

I pushed through the crowd, advancing slowly. I never said thank you. I left, and that was the last time I saw you.

Aah!

You told me, didn't you? That in fifteen years, there'd be the fiftieth anniversary celebration of Ruirui's enthronement, the descendant of the royal family currently wearing the crown. You said criminals might be pardoned then. It had been exactly fifteen years. Did you spend all those years alone, buried deep underground in the cannery of that far-off town? And then you were finally dug up from the earth, let out of the barrel, and you went looking for me. Tonight, you found me, you came to see me. Talked to me, pretending to ask for directions…

Did you believe with your uncomplicated heart that we would smile at each other and delight in our reunion? For a Bamboo, the memory would have been like yesterday, after all.

You. That day long ago, you…

Who on earth are you?

"Heeey!" I called the girl, idiotically. "It's you, isn't it? It's me! I can remember. I know I can remember. So just hold on. Heey! Heeey…"

Heeey…

The crowd in front of the station only grew larger. For the briefest moment, I thought I saw an empty sleeve flapping in the summer wind, but I quickly lost sight of it.

I ran. Sweating, I kept looking for her. But she was already nowhere to be found, this ghost of the past who had come to me for a fleeting moment on a summer day fifteen years after the fact.

Her voice came back to me, so intent on that long-ago evening: *Weird! But we were having so much fun together every night!*

♦ ♦ ♦

Bamboo...

Bamboo don't change. They keep thinking the whole time. Throughout their long lives, the whole time. They don't get older, so the nature of their thinking doesn't change either. It wasn't the Bamboo. No. It was the humans who actually forgot that they had been close.

I finally understood what the two gentle Bamboo had told me back then.

Our dream is for you to grow up and live. And it doesn't matter a bit if you get busy and naturally forget all this about having lived with some weird grass monsters. Because that is in itself growing up, living and changing.

I stood frozen in the throng and bustle, watching the vision of the girl departing, feeling at my wit's end as I watched the last traces of the past glittering and disappearing. And then I started slowly walking in the opposite direction. I staggered and stumbled in my sadness and shame.

I was fairly late by the time I showed up at the restaurant where my friends were gathered. My fiancée was sick of waiting for me and looked up with relief at my arrival.

"Sorry I'm late." I smiled. "Sorry, guys."

They raised their voices in welcome, and I was suddenly relieved. *Aah*, I thought, with a pain in my heart, still feeling the same shame at myself as before I'd stepped into the restaurant.

I had to at least cherish this now. That was all I could do. I had promised to live. To change. To never give up. That day…

My Bamboo, supposedly more precious to me than anything. Aah, that day…

Kyo! Humans are fire!

One of my friends started a toast. Glasses were clinked. A bus drove by outside, rocking from side to side. I heard the sound of the engine. The taillights shone hazily, but it passed by soon enough, and it grew dark again.

Aah. But…your… What's your name? Aah…

And then, just like the buses that roared as they drove by the restaurant, time passed. Years in the blink of an eye.

FACE

*K*rnch. Krnch. The soles of my leather shoes on the ground. My head was hanging, my eyes resting on the tips of those shoes. The hot, dry sand swallowed my feet and released them again. Sweat on my temples ran down the back of my neck. I could hear the crashing of the waves from the ocean behind me. The merciless summer sun felt like it would melt anything and everything.

"There it is! The cottage there!" The young man was a

little ahead of me, but now he stopped and stretched a hand out slowly, pointing.

I squinted. And there it was, that familiar house, a distant mirage in the summer afternoon. Aah, it hadn't changed at all. Or maybe it was a bit weathered by wind and rain; the color seemed like it had faded. Or maybe it was just that I remembered it wrong.

A sign was stabbed into the ground at an angle, FOR RENT in big red letters.

I smiled slowly, sinking into the sand.

I stepped timidly onto the wooden terrace once so familiar to me. Grains of sand were stuck to it, but the wooden bench where the two young men had so often sat next to each other was exactly as it had been.

"Well, it *is* an old building. But the price is very reasonable for just that reason. I'll open it up now! Whoops! The fitting's a bit off, hmm? Have to get that fixed… Oh! The former residents just left everything behind—furniture, boxes, a whole bunch of stuff. If you wanted to rent the place, though, of course we'd take care of all of that for you… Wait, what?"

"I said, it's fine the way it is. You don't have to throw anything out. I'll take it."

"Really! Hmm, this place?" The young real estate agent looked up at me curiously. Perhaps he was starting to think that this tall older man was actually a mysterious character.

I laughed quietly for him. "The truth is, when I was a boy, I used to live around here. I left when I was seventeen, but when you hit my age, you suddenly get homesick. Or maybe it's just nostalgia, you know? Ha ha! At any rate, seniors can't exactly pay a fortune in rent, either, hmm?"

"What? Around here?"

"Mm-hmm. Back then, we had all these prefab houses crammed together in that empty lot, you know? It was an elementary and junior high school. I suppose it's long gone, though."

"Oh, no, it's still there!" The man suddenly grew overly familiar and came closer. A cloud-free smile popped up on his face. "I went to school there too. So you're an alumnus, hmm?"

"Oh! Looks like we have something in common then."

We smiled brightly at each other. The lease was proffered, and I accepted it. We went inside.

My heart suddenly started pounding wildly. The living room was basically unchanged from the way it had been back then. The same sofa and table. The bookshelf. Only the wall clock was different; the hands were frozen, motionless.

"Hmm? What's the matter?"

"Oh, nothing." I shook my head. I noticed the exaggerated look of surprise on the young man's face, as though he were worried that the mysterious old man might collapse and die right then and there. I grinned reassuringly and then breathed deeply to calm my heart. I sat down on the dusty sofa and spread the lease out before me.

Beyond the glass doors, the dazzling summer light. The glittering blue ocean. The waves echoed invitingly.

✦ ✦ ✦

After that night, I made my fiancée an official member of my family register. Eventually, we had a single child, a boy. I was put in charge of a new branch of the cake shop, and I moved my family to a bedroom town. Our son grew up, got a job, started his own family.

I was past sixty now. One day—well, last winter, our son decided to take us on a trip in the name of filial piety. But I had work that clashed with the dates of the trip, and I was forced to stay home. So he and his mother flew alone together to Shanghai, since it was the time of year when the famed hairy crab was at peak deliciousness. There was an accident. A large something, a bird, possibly, flew into the engine of the commercial plane they had boarded. The airplane dropped into the ocean between Japan and China. Almost nothing was recovered.

I had two grandchildren, but my son's wife and her parents took them in. Around the same time, I was diagnosed with an incurable illness, a disease which appeared to be slowly advancing. How much longer would I be able to keep fighting?

So I decided to move. The people who had pursued me in the past—be it the organization in the town above or the Bamboo government—had likely long forgotten about me, after all these years. In which case, I figured I would go back to the town where I had lived so long ago. And I ended up renting this beloved cottage. The lease was signed in no time at all.

This would most likely be my last residence.

❖ ❖ ❖

Now, the following morning, I brought over my very few belongings and moved in right away. I had breakfast, and then I rolled up my sleeves and got to work cleaning the dust-covered floor.

It appeared that my Bamboo had left abruptly, taking basically nothing with him. What on earth had happened, I wondered. A foreboding feeling flitted through my heart; maybe he had long ago departed from this world. But when I went into the small interior room, the large wooden chest that should have been there was the only thing missing. So I reframed the situation. He was still in this world, he had just moved away. Probably someplace far away.

Other than the chest, though, pretty much everything was where it should have been. Even the candlesticks of assorted designs placed throughout the room.

I neatly wiped away the dust piled up on the furniture and casually opened the cupboard, where I got a surprise. The old cameras were all still there. Together with a neat pile of 8 mm camera film spools. I slowly reached out and picked one up. And then my eyes fell on another spool.

Abruptly, it felt like a hand was squeezing my heart tightly. Written on the spool was "KYO'S HERE!" in magic marker.

I went and looked for the projector I was sure was in the interior room. My hands started to shake.

In the smaller room, dim in the evening light, I got ready to project the film onto the unfinished, dirty wall in place of a screen—and then stopped. I needed some time to prepare myself mentally. I made some tea, drank it, made another cup, and drank that down too before I finally stood up again.

I went back to the projector. I reached a hand out. The film started rolling, clacking away. I leaned against a pillar and watched closely with nervous eyes at a vision from the past.

A young man with pale skin and a shy, thoughtful look appeared on-screen. I groaned. Yoji.

In the back of my mind, I saw again Yoji's face in profile, burning, bathed in the light of the morning sun. *Accept everything.* His voice filled my ears. My back still up against the pillar, my body jerked liked I had just been punched hard in the gut. The memory of my crime on that distant day came rushing back. I mustered up my courage and turned intently back to the screen.

Oh! I was stunned to see how young he had been. Much younger than my own son, of course. He looked somewhere between boy and man, didn't he? I had relied on him so completely, so wholeheartedly, back then, this youth with his thin lines. It seemed funny to me now.

The camera moved down to the young man's feet. And then, there...there was a little boy. I reeled in shock once more. The boy's limbs were skinny and fine, and he looked pale.

This...what was this?

Objectively speaking, he was not at all cute. I couldn't find any special appeal in him. Huh. So I was once nothing more than one of those surly children you so often see? An uncomfortable doubt grew in my heart. Why would they go out of their way to save the life of this dull child? Why had they risked such danger for him? And why had they loved him the way they did?

Yoji jokingly pretended to bite my neck. And quickly stopped, like he was embarrassed. The look on his face was so shy, so kindhearted. He slowly lifted his head. He looked this way and said something as he stretched out a slender arm.

Ohh, he's changing places with the cameraman.

A bearded young man with large, jet-black eyes and dark skin appeared. Unblinking, I stared at the figure of my former Bamboo. He too was incredibly young. He looked almost childish. With an innocent smile on his face, he grabbed me and tossed me up toward the ceiling. A shrill laugh was ripped out of me. My voice wasn't at all endearing, either. It sounded hysterical, an unpleasant din.

But he, my old Bamboo—he alone dazzled the eye each time he laughed, his face shining. In this scene from my past, the Bamboo were beautiful. And I was an ugly child.

Hey, Mustah? Yoji? Back then. Why…did you love me?

Klak, klak, klak. The projector sounded dull somehow.

Finally, the film ended. I let out a long breath. A mysterious pain lingered deep in my heart. As if a long period of time I could never get back had run right by me.

That night, thoroughly exhausted, I took my medicine, and I had no sooner sat down on the sofa than I was fast asleep.

The sofa was sweetly familiar, a fond memory. I had used it as a bed when I was a child. I had slept here with my feet sticking out even after I had started high school and had grown too tall for it. And now too, when I abruptly woke in the middle of the night, I found I had rolled over so that my legs were dangling from the knees down against the side of the sofa, feet on the floor.

I had woken up to the sound of someone apparently coming into the house. It was summer, but I felt a cold breeze on my face. I suddenly called out the names of my wife and son. *Is it you? Are you here?* But perhaps I only thought the dead had come for me because I was tired and still half-asleep. I opened my eyes and looked around, but there was no one there, of course. I was alone.

Well, whatever. I'll just take it slow.

I fell once more into a deep sleep.

✦ ✦ ✦

One day, rather belatedly, I realized that there was no clock among the meager possessions I'd brought with me, and I looked around, troubled.

I reached out to the old wall clock, frozen in a moment in time ever since who knew when. Now that I was an adult, my hand reached it easily. I adjusted the dusty thing and carefully wound it. The clock groaned unpleasantly, and then the hands started to move once more. I was overcome by the strange feeling that time wasn't flowing into the future, but rather returning to the past with each *tic* of those hands. But it wasn't a bad feeling. Unconsciously, I laughed silently.

I let my gaze wander casually over the pillar I had been leaning against. It felt like the clock had triggered some memory from the past.

Oh! I realized what it was. I crouched down on the spot and looked quietly at the marks on the surface of the pillar. Several horizontal lines. The day and year written in marker. The lowest mark was somewhere between my chest and my stomach.

Aah. The youthful voices of the Bamboo shouting in

delight. They got so carried away as they measured me. I was so little back then. I could almost see the scene before me again, like it had also been restored to me in the 8 mm film.

I got to my knees and hung my head helplessly. I stared out of the corner of my eye. Had I really been that little? It was such a long time ago. I stroked the pillar endlessly with the palm of my hand.

I had felt confused, uncertain, the day I returned to the cottage, but over the past few days, those feelings had started to shift into something more peaceful. Each time these bits of the past drew close and gently wound around me, I was embraced by a familiar fondness and a distant love.

The waves sounded out as if to encourage me.

I got used to my life alone in the cottage. Eating through my meager savings, I read books, listened to music. I went to the hospital, got my medicine, came home.

Perhaps increasingly worried about the old man out on the coast, the young man from the real estate agency would check in on me from time to time. "Are you doing all right here?" He told me various things about the area whenever he stopped by, and it seemed that, both above and below, the towns were as they had been. That is to say, both were full of fighting. I supposed that the humans grew old and were just replaced one after another with new faces, while the town itself didn't change much.

I baked cake and cookies for when he'd come by, and he took them home gladly. I guess he gave them to his mother. A friend removed in age—I'm not sure if I could call him that, but, well, he was nice to have around.

"It really isn't safe around here. Make sure you lock your doors… That said, though, it doesn't really look like there's much here to steal, eh?"

"There's not. Ha ha ha!"

"And you just laugh. You really are easygoing, huh?"

"I don't have anything to protect anymore. That'll make a person easygoing, you know? Oh, that reminds me. How's your mom doing?"

"Good. Oh! That cake, she really liked it. Says she'd happily have more of it."

"I can do that. I'll bake another one for her."

I wondered how many more years—no, months I'd be able to keep living here like this?

Either way, time gently flowed on.

◆ ◆ ◆

And then, one night after two weeks or so. One fateful night.

I was sleeping on the sofa again. I had to force myself in there at an angle, which left my legs from the knees down dangling over the side. The sound of the waves outside was comforting. The ticking of the wall clock, functional once again, wasn't too bad either.

Wait. There was another noise.

It came from the terrace. I cocked my head to the side, wondering if it was a burglar. It was, after all, a dangerous neighborhood. Plenty of people were cruelly killed for the bit of cash they had.

I didn't want to deal with it. And for a while, I kept lying on the sofa, but eventually I got up reluctantly. And I saw a skinny girl in a summer school uniform standing like a ghost on the other side of the glass.

I blinked in surprise. I wasn't scared. On the contrary, she looked like someone I knew well, and I even felt a deep affection.

"Nako? Sister?"

For a moment, I thought perhaps my ride from the other side had come for me.

But there was no answer.

I strained my eyes. Long hair hanging down past her shoulders, very shy eyes. She was stepping from one foot to the other, like something was upsetting her. From the look of her, she was still only thirteen or fourteen. I looked closely at her face.

No, I didn't know this girl. This wasn't my sister's ghost.

The fog gradually cleared from my half-asleep brain. "What's wrong? Are you lost?" I asked, gently.

Thinking about it, there was no way a girl in uniform could walk around safely by herself in a neighborhood this bad, this late at night. Which meant I was dealing with someone mysterious. I could be in danger if I carelessly opened the door. But I was already old, with not much longer left to me, and it seemed foolish somehow for a grown man to be afraid of a lone girl.

I stood up. I unlocked the glass doors and slid them open. I peered at the girl's face. "Where'd you come from?"

The girl averted her eyes. She looked back and stared toward the darkness where the ocean spread out behind the house. Following her gaze, I turned my eyes that way as well, but of course there was no one there.

The summer night was humid and hot. The sandy beach held the day's heat and shimmered slightly like a mirage. The light of the moon was very beautiful. A quiet night. The sound of the waves alone eased the heart. It was a good night to die. I wasn't afraid.

I peered at the girl's face again and offered her a joking smile. "Are you maybe a Bamboo? Something like that?"

"*I* am!" The answer came from the darkness.

I gasped and lifted my face.

Instantly, the girl turned on her heel and ran into the night. Her slender retreating figure shuddered violently, threatening to snap in half.

Aah, just now was... That was a voice I could never forget.

I was stunned into silence. And then I smiled slowly. I waited for him to come out of the darkness.

The young man strode up to the terrace lazily and stopped. The girl hid fearfully behind him and stared up at me.

I looked closely. At a glance, I could tell he was a lone stray Bamboo. He stood leaning to one side, but in a way that made it seem like he didn't actually realize he was off-kilter. His dark skin was now jet-black with filth. His black hair was disheveled, tangled like a rat's nest. His beard was gray with all the dust and dirt stuck to it. His clothes were also a disaster. Buried under layers of shirts and vests and coats, he looked like a mountain of old rags.

The many days since that night!

He was the only partner for me. So, from now on, well, I'll just go it alone. His voice, trying so hard to be bright, flooded my ears.

I staggered into a run, nothing like the energetic dashes

I'd managed back then, though. My legs got tangled up. Lurching, I managed to make it to him somehow. I reached out and hugged him. If he were a vision, he would have turned into white mist and disappeared the instant I touched him. I wouldn't have been the least bit surprised if he had. It was that kind of night.

But he stayed in my arms, solid. The scent of bamboo tickled my nostrils. I tried to speak, and of course all I could do was say his name. "Aah, Mustah…"

"So you came back, huh, little Kyo!"

"Mustah! Mustah! Mustah!"

"I knew last week. I came to visit one night, and I saw you sleeping there. And then I couldn't decide whether or not we should actually meet. But, you know…"

"You knew I was back? You should've come and seen me right away! I wanted to look for you, Mustah! But it's not like a human would be able to tell me where to find a Bamboo. Oh!" I surprised myself and clapped a hand over my mouth. Because I had reverted to speaking like a girl again. It was as if, in the very instant of this reunion, that long-gone time had come rushing back to me.

I stared into his eyes. They were gentle, playful. He looked filthy, but his skin was as young as ever, his physique was exactly the same. Bamboo really didn't age.

I suddenly became ashamed and started fidgeting. "I've gotten really old, huh? Mustah, don't stare at me so much."

"You turned out wonderfully, Kyo!" His voice swelled with pride.

I gasped and looked back at him. Now that I thought about it, he had watched over me in the film like I was so adorable he could hardly stand it, despite the fact that I was objectively a dull, small child. And that day we parted too, he kept telling me how I was a very special flame to them. So then, did I look like a special, wonderful something to Mustah's eyes alone, even now?

"I'm a flame on the verge of going out."

"A flame's a flame! And, like..."

"Hmm?"

"Kyo, you kept your promise to me!" He looked up at me. In the middle of that dirty face, his beautiful eyes shone like stars. He reached out a hand and poked my head. It was the sort of thing you'd do to a small child. He grinned playfully. "You fought, huh, boyo? Just looking at you, I can tell. Yeah?"

I nodded slowly. "Yeah!" I was glad I was alive, I was glad I'd been born, I was glad I'd come back here.

✦ ✦ ✦

I invited them both into the living room. The girl quickly devoured the cookie I offered her and then flopped down onto the sofa the way I used to, curled up, and fell asleep, as though she was completely exhausted.

"Oh!" Mustah found the 8 mm camera and turned the lens on me and the girl, cocking his head to one side as if wondering whether it still worked. And it did appear to be filming. I turned the camera on him then, and he grinned, embarrassed.

"The truth is, I have a favor to ask, Kyo."

The small hours of the night. I was sitting on the floor across from Mustah, wiping the dirt off his skin, combing his hair. I also found a clean black shirt and put it on him. And some pants, although they were long enough to fit my lanky legs, so I had to roll them up twice for him. Gradually, he began to look the way I remembered him, and I saw that he was utterly unchanged, the same as he'd always been, like we'd parted only yesterday.

"A favor?" Somewhere in my heart, I was instinctively afraid. And then I swallowed that feeling down. "You can ask me anything. Go ahead!"

"My secret got out, y'know?"

"Oh! This girl?"

"Yeah."

"She's human, right?" I said in a quiet voice, turning my eyes on the sofa.

"You knew?"

"Well, it's just when I offered her a cookie, she ate it, didn't she? No matter which way you slice it, she's a hungry human child." *Just like I used to be, eh?* I added in my heart.

Mustah scratched his face, troubled. "I just sort of took her in. She was about to be killed, and there wasn't a home she could go back to anymore. But I figured killer and victim were both humans, so that was that, and I was going to leave them be and fly off, y'know? But then, Kyo, I suddenly remembered you. Like, I sort of saw you in her."

The girl rolled over in her sleep. Mustah hung his head, his face growing darker.

"But it's totally not doable by myself. The only reason I managed to hide you and bring you up back then, Kyo, was because I had Yoji. I really get that now. They found out pretty quick, y'know?"

"Found out? Mustah…"

"Yeah." There was resignation in his voice. "Ruirui's guys came after us tonight."

I said nothing but simply stared at him. Mustah looked straight into my eyes.

I vividly remembered the terror of that night, suddenly surrounded by more than ten Bamboo, male and female. And that face, Yoji bound by chains, left out in the morning light, burning to death, his charred face growing ever smaller. I shuddered. No one could ever completely escape them. The Bamboo government was relentless.

Mustah was… Then…

"Can I maybe ask you to take care of her, Kyo?" His voice was calm.

"You can." I nodded immediately.

"Are you sure?"

"Of course, Mustah!"

Until the girl was eighteen. Maybe four or five years. Could I keep going that long?

The only thing to do was to do it. I was still alive, after all. My flame had flickered to near nothing, but I'd fan it as best I could and keep going for a little while, albeit slowly. Until my final day.

After staring at my face for a while, Mustah grinned at me, relieved. His smile was the same as always, carefree, almost like cheerfulness itself. The bright innocence and enthusiasm of my Bamboo. I had yearned for him every day back then. My heart was full again. I pushed all these emotions back.

"The girl will be all right. But what will happen to you, Mustah? Will you…run?"

"Nah, I probably won't be able to escape."

"So then they'll catch you. My voice was miserable again, like it had been back then.

"They won't catch me!"

"What?"

"If it's between that and being burned at the stake by them, I'll go on my own terms."

"On your own terms. You can't mean…"

"Yeah." Mustah's face grew quiet. "If it means them catching me and burning me alive like Yoji, then I'll do it myself. I mean, like, I've always made decisions about myself on my own, y'know?"

"B-but—"

"A Bamboo's life's not forever, right? It ends at some point. So I don't mind a bit if that some point is dawn today."

"Mustah…" I swallowed hard and watched over his profile.

"Look, Kyo. The night's almost over." Mustah pointed straight at the eastern sky.

The pitch-black ocean was steadily shifting to indigo. A new day was trying to come over from the other side. For me, another day in what was left of my life, not much different from any other. For the girl, it was certainly a wonderful, unknown time. And for the Bamboo, a mere instant, a clipping from a long succession of decades.

The sun would come up!

Soon.

Dawn!

Mustah laughed finally, as if to bolster his courage. He didn't look sad or like he was suffering. He really was the same old Mustah.

Unable to stand it, I started crying, like I had returned to being a boy of ten. I was happy he had come to see me in the end, but it was too awful that he was going to die. That I would see both Bamboo vanish from this world. They should have long outlived me, these Bamboo, eternally young men, so dazzling I almost hated it, and me, a wrinkled old man. There was no way this was right.

A cold palm stroked my head gently. In my ear, I heard, "I am seriously one lucky Bamboo to get to see you again in the end, my little Kyo!"

As he stood, Mustah was the beautiful, charming young man of days gone by. Endlessly enthusiastic, always playing. Sitting on the ground next to him, I was already old, old enough to be his father, his grandfather.

He walked slowly out onto the terrace. His feet clacked against the wood. I watched him slump down onto the bench. It was the same artless gesture I had seen so often back then, the way he walked over and sat there. He used to welcome me home from school, chat with Yoji beside him about something or other. Sometimes, he would sit there with me, holding my hand amiably, and talk about school. I'd thought that he alone would never change.

He looked back at me and waved innocently. His lips moved in the shape of "Goodbye."

The eastern sky gradually grew brighter.

I stood up and slowly went out onto the terrace. Mustah looked up at me in surprise. I sat down heavily next to him, like I so often had when I came home from school.

"Let me be here too. Please, Mustah."

Hey. It's okay, right? My Bamboo. Please.

He nodded like he had no choice. "But, like, it won't look too good, y'know? I mean, I *am* going to burn."

Shivering, I remembered that burning, shrinking face. "I know."

"You do…? Oh, that's right!"

"I want to be with you. Um, okay, I…"

I've always loved you. Ever since I was ten years old. The truth is, I never wanted to let anyone else have you. Not a man, not a woman, not Yoji, not some stranger. No one but me.

Half a century has passed since then, and now here I am, finally alone with you.

But I couldn't put that into words. Even now, at this age, my feelings for Mustah were too hot, too chaotic. Love, sadness, hatred, pain, and yet so blessed. Alive, it was like my own small face was crumpling, burning with the heat of an invisible love.

Silently, I leaned my head on his shoulder. And then hurriedly pulled it up again. I was worried that I might put that troubled look back on his face. But when I glanced at his profile, he was smiling, carefree. I was relieved from the bottom of my heart.

"Hey. Hey, Mustah?"

"What? Are you a little kid now?"

"…I'll get to see you again soon, right?"

Right…Mustah. In that place. In the peaceful sky. We get to see all the people who've gone before us again, right?

Mustah. Yoji. My sister. Mr. Yu. My wife. My son. My first love. Niita. All the people I'd loved.

And then I was sure I'd be able to say all the things I never could before. Apologies, words of love, appreciation. Tell

them how I'd missed them. It wo
thing. There'd be no sin I couldn't
to see them again.

At some point, the time came f
go out. And what if, on that day, t
sky…

Now, with the passage of time,
Otherwise, it was too much to have
lost too much. In the past, and now

Mustah finally grinned at me.
again!"

"Mustah, Mustah, Mustah!" I si

"Ha ha!" He laughed fondly, slov
we'll say goodbye for a little while
thank you. For coming to us. For
happy. For showing us your wonde
up our frozen days. For calling me y
take care, Kyo, hon. I love you too,
pens, you're my son, my best friend,

Dawn began to break.

"So, basically, you were just one hi

"Mustah. Mustah, I love you!" I fi

He laughed delightedly. "Me too, l

◆◆◆

At last, the sun rose up over the horiz

2.
I CAME TO SHOW YOU REAL FLOWERS

PEACH

It was me. I did it.
  Little old me.
  No one knows.

(Since then. A hundred years.)

◆ ◆ ◆

The fog's thick tonight. A good night for hunting!
  I stood atop the telephone pole on one leg and looked down on the road below. The flashing lights. The downtown back alleys. Everything stained and sooty.

A golden cat raced by, a stray. It was of a foreign breed and had probably been pretty expensive. A man and a woman strolled past it from the other direction. A sleepy-looking middle-aged man and a skinnyish girl wearing glasses. The man was saying something. The girl nodded at the right moment and lifted her eyes my way for a second. A winter wind blew and set her scarf flapping uneasily.

That gust pushed the fog away, and the moonlight from above threw me into sharp relief on top of the telephone pole—a girl standing on one leg, a scarecrow. I winked and waved saucily with my right hand at the girl below. I didn't have a left arm, so the sleeve of my coat fluttered emptily.

When her eyes found me, Momo—"peach"—nodded with what looked like relief. Her lips moved. *Ma. Ri. Ka.*

The gusts of air carried with them the hustle and bustle of the main street, the flirting lilts of the girls, the rough sing-song of the drunks. Pounding music wound its way toward us. The honking of an irritated driver.

I'm jumping! The wind roared in my ears. *Sudden drop! Night bird style!* I had been living for more than a hundred years as a Bamboo, so I was used to this by now.

From behind, I swept down toward the strange man walking alongside Momo. Going into stealth mode, even my breath subsonic, I flew in at a low altitude, almost crawling forward, my belly scraping air. My long black hair flew up like a mane around me. The hem of my trailing black coat flapped and fluttered, the cloak of the god of death herself.

"…Having lived this long, I think human beings…life is a series of choices…I don't regret anything…But…sometimes, well." The man was speaking passionately about something.

I drew in quite close, nodding slyly with a serious look on my face. Seeing me, Momo sneered secretly from behind her black-framed glasses. A small smile, malicious and mischievous, but somehow timid.

"I have no regrets, but…I guess it was just after I turned forty. I started thinking that life gets revenge on you for the choices you made in the past. Like, if you hadn't done this that time, it would've turned out like this, you know? Every day was like that."

"You said before," Momo replied, in a quiet voice, "that you didn't go out with anyone in high school."

"Yeah. I thought I was fine with that. But now, that choice is really getting its revenge. Which is why I'm doing this with a young girl like you," he said, turning back toward Momo.

And then, in the blink of an eye, a third head between their two. He finally noticed my presence and took a sharp breath. Whatever else I might be, I'm Bamboo, so I offered up a creepy smile, very aware of my monstrous appearance.

The man stared at me, long and hard. He then looked at Momo, comparing my face with her suddenly demure look. "Ha?" He let out a shallow breath.

I'm way cuter than Momo. My eyes are wide in the center, round, with a particularly sharp outline. Before all this happened to me, I was probably not bad looking. But now the tip of my nose had been shaved into a pointed blade, two small holes peeking out from below, and when the wind picked my hair up, you could see my left ear had also been cut off, gone forever. My left arm had been ripped off too. I don't show up in mirrors, so I haven't seen myself in a while, but when I show myself like this, pretty much everyone...

"Unh! Aaaaaaaah!"

...screams like that, so I'm fairly certain I'm pretty frightening now. Although Momo seemed fine with the way I looked. Maybe she was just used to it, though.

The man pitched forward, almost falling in his attempt at escape. I watched him go, still hovering about twenty centimeters off the ground. I mean, this kind of thrill's the whole point of the hunt! Beside me, Momo yawned very deliberately as if to make that point. I guess it was already time for her to go to bed. That yawn was basically like she was telling me not to have fun with this, to just hurry up. So I'd better get to it, then.

I kicked at the air and flew. I stretched out my right

arm and left leg. Sudden ascent! And then sudden descent, spinning at high speed, tumbling! *Thwk!* I landed in front of the running man, and I slowly looked back at him, the hem of my long coat flapping.

The man looked even more surprised, almost like a small child, an innocent. His face said he couldn't believe this was happening to him. He hadn't done anything wrong. He believed that nothing bad could ever happen to him.

A hundred years since then. And I'll never get used to seeing it. I can't help but get excited. The look on his face. In his eyes. Dear God. It's like I'll never be able to tear my eyes away from this. A hundred years, and still…

I sprang up and perched like a bird on his solid shoulder. I chopped my heel into the back of his neck, bringing it down like a judge's gavel. The man crumpled to the ground with a thud.

The ephemeral flickering of the electric lights. The alley of the shopping district. The foggy night. Cold. Cold. Very.

Momo approached sluggishly, took the man's wrist, stuck the needle in, almost bored with the familiarity of the act, and drew out the arterial blood. The syringe comically large, like our bodies had gotten smaller.

The man grew pale. "Unnh," he groaned, regaining consciousness. "W-why kill me? If it's my wallet…take it!"

"Yes. Naturally, we'll also be accepting your wallet," Momo said, calmly. She was so collected, a doctor in the making.

"What…are you doing?"

"Well, we're taking your blood."

"…What?"

"Five hundred milliliters."

"W-why?"

"Oh, we simply must have it," Momo said, giggling softly. She was having fun, a mischievous child up to no good. Adopting a singsong tone, she chanted, "Weee are a paaaair of wannabeeeee gods of death. That. Is. Why!"

I heard quiet footsteps from a ways off. Men, from the sounds of it. Several of them. Young voices laughing. Carefree, fooling around. Maybe they were drunk.

I met Momo's eyes, and we nodded to one another. She pulled the heavy syringe up and tossed it into the rucksack on her back. A motion she, too, was used to now. The rucksack sank heavily and bit into her overly slender shoulders, almost cruelly.

Momo stood up and looked down on the man. "Catch! And..."

"Release!" I finished.

My voice was husky and old, in stark opposition with my face, totally different from Momo's vibrant, youthful tones. Here alone, my age showed through. After all, I'd made it past the hundred-year mark and was still alive. The same as always. Forever immature.

The men turned the corner and came into view. Kicking at the air with my right foot, I planted my left foot hard on the man's back. It was like I was kicking a soccer ball toward the goal. His body danced up into space. I held Momo on one side with my right arm, and she suddenly giggled soundlessly—a childish coolness to show that she wouldn't be impressed no matter what she saw. Her heart wouldn't be moved; she had decided life was nothing. Swallowed up by the fog, we—a pair of would-be gods of death—disappeared.

The men noticed the human figure on the ground and stopped. One of them looked up our way. Momo shuddered in my arm, and I panicked, ascending rapidly. *To space!* Cold, cold space. Dark blue. The chill air of night crept into the two caves of my sculpted nose, and a single tear spilled from my eyes.

+ + +

We rested briefly on the roof of an old mixed-use building, alighting like little birds. Momo pulled the heavy syringe out of her rucksack and handed it to me ever so carefully. Then she sat formally on her knees and set out for herself a triangle sandwich and a can of coffee purchased at a convenience store.

Supper alone, together. A night like any other. I relaxed and sat down, cross-legged, before drinking the blood. I'm an elderly Bamboo, after all. I can't keep going the way I used to.

"Hey. We should get going, you know?"

The words came at me, and I gasped. A serious chunk of time had gone by. I staggered to my feet.

Momo, always the considerate one, decided we should take the stairs down to the ground instead of flying. Each floor had a bar on it, and the laughter and flirtations of the people inside wafted out to us in the stairwell, riding a wave of music.

Momo hung her head sadly. We couldn't go through any of the doors. I mean, no one was waiting for us inside or anything.

"What should we do, Marika?" she asked, once we were outside again.

"What do you want to do?"

"Huh? It's up to you. You're the boss of me, after all."

"Okay, then. How 'bout we head out to a different town?" I grinned as I showed her the wallet I'd taken from the man's coat pocket.

The tension drained out of her. She looked relieved somehow.

"What? What's up?"

"You'll take me, right, Marika? However far away, wherever you go. You'll take me, right?"

"Of course." I was baffled. "What's going on in your head, Momo? For starters, how would I lure my prey without you? I keep telling you, I need you too."

"Good." Momo started walking again, swaggering a little now.

I staggered after her, hiding my nose under a surgical mask, the kind you wear when you have a cold. Turning toward the station, we held hands as we walked down the main road, the seductive voices of women flirting and the music from the various bars growing louder, vying to drown the other out.

✦ ✦ ✦

Momo's been with me for the last six months. Before she came along, I'd been alone for a while.

Long hidden away in a mountainous region of China, Bamboo are monsters of the giant grass, botanical vampires. We live by drinking human blood. After a time, those original Bamboo were driven out of their idyllic, isolated village deep in the mountains, the kind of place found in the old Chinese fable "Peach Blossom Spring," and criminals and whatnot were among the Bamboo who eventually drifted all the way to this island country. They hid themselves here and there, occasionally attacking humans.

When I was fifteen, a Bamboo killed my family, but he didn't quite manage to finish me off, and I was the only one to live, infected as one of them. It'd been nearly a hundred years since then. Now I was a Bamboo through and through. A Bamboo uncomfortable with other Bamboo. A monster all alone.

It was almost a coincidence that I met Momo. I wanted to light some incense for a friend who'd died—a human—so I went to the wake. He and I went way back; he's the reason I look the way I do now, scarred within an inch of my life. His house was in some impoverished and corrupt village at the tip of a certain peninsula. When I got there, I found his adopted daughter—a high school girl he'd taken in and raised as best he could—huddled up in one corner of the room, sobbing pathetically, naked, her body covered in bites, cuts, and traces of blood.

Momo.

At the time, I'd never even imagined we'd become close. I simply looked at her out of the corner of my eye and silently lit the incense. In that town, danger was a matter of course; it was unthinkable that a child or a girl of marriageable age could live there without anyone in her corner. And now that Momo's adoptive father was dead, she needed someone to watch out for her sooner rather than later. I rolled my eyes. That's just how it was in that town.

I'd flown into the room, so Momo was naturally surprised. She kept her eyes on me through her tears.

"Um!" When I moved to leave, a trembling voice called out as if to stop me. "Are you a Bamboo?"

"You know the Bamboo?" I looked back, and Momo was smiling, almost flirtatiously, despite the fact that she'd been crying up until that moment.

Her parents had never been a part of her life, and an incident in the house that had taken her in left Momo alive, and alone, and then scooped up by another Bamboo man. This Bamboo had then asked a human he trusted to become her adoptive father. So she had made it this far in life because there were people of all kinds helping her. Left to her own devices, Momo would have died long ago.

Momo was weak. And because she was weak, she was pretty good at latching on to people who appeared to be strong. She followed me silently, without so much as a glance back at the home of the adoptive father who had done so much for her.

Our situations were oddly similar, and we were about the same age in appearance. When she started to walk beside me, I got the feeling we might get along. It was the first time I'd had a girl by my side, but I got used to it pretty quick.

And now it had already been six months.

◆ ◆ ◆

We got on the night bus and huddled together in a ball in a corner seat.

"Go to sleep, Momo!"

Momo nodded. When she was sleepy, she was as docile as a child. She took off her glasses and put them in the pocket of her gray duffle coat.

Our seat was dark. The bus was full but quiet, like all the other passengers were ghosts. A bus that ferried the dead.

Cold. Cold. Me and my body that generated no warmth. And hadn't for a hundred years now. Me, a girl who had died ages ago that night. A member of the walking dead. Momo fell back in the seat as if she were the dead one. Her warmth came through to me, and I shivered.

Momo.

Momo was alive. She was living, a life always right beside me. Maybe that made me happy, but being happy was dangerous.

"Hey, Marika?"

Daybreak was approaching. I could hear the soft breathing and snores of the people asleep on the bus. They slept easily, unaware of the Bamboo in their midst. The red taillights of the cars in front of us flickered like will-o'-the-wisps. It was still chilly inside the bus.

"Marika?"

"Hmm?"

"Stay with me always, okay?" Momo whispered in my ear. "Marika. Marikaaaa. I don't want you to disappear on me! I mean, like, when I think about me sleeping all nice and sound like this, and then one night I wake up and you're gone, I get so anxious."

"Yeah, yeah…"

"You're the only one…who knows…"

"Huh?"

"What happened to me."

"Ohh, that?"

"I mean, I'm never going to tell anyone else my whole life!"

"But what'll you do if you fall in love? Won't you have to be honest with them?"

"I won't. I won't tell." Marika opened her narrow eyes and shook her head stubbornly. "I won't tell. I won't."

"Mm."

"I won't. I won't."

"Mm."

"I mean, if I never tell, then someday…it'll be like…it never happened…maybe."

"Yeah?"

"No way! It'll never be like it never happened. But you'll know, Marika," Momo said, her voice trembling. "You'll remember for me. Immortal Bamboo…you'll save me."

The bus shook even more fiercely. I sat up. "But Bamboo aren't immortal."

"What?"

"I told you. We live around 120 years. I figure I've got a little over ten years left. And just like bamboo, bam! In the end, we bloom these beautiful white flowers, and then it's all over."

"No!" Momo exclaimed, quietly. Uneasy tears rose up in her eyes, like a child. "Don't die!"

"I told you—we don't die, we disappear."

"Marikaaaa, that's so scary."

"Well, when the time comes, I'll show you some real flowers!" I said with a sneer.

Momo sulked for a while, all "I don't want you to," but eventually, she murmured, "Okay, then promise me. For sure, okay?" and dropped quickly into sleep again.

We reached the next town before dawn. We stayed in an old business hotel, and after closing the windows up tightly, Momo set up the simple blackout tent she kept in her rucksack for me. I slipped inside. I felt her presence outside, and I closed my eyes.

"Night, Marika."

"Night…Momo."

Switch. Now it was my turn to sleep.

◆ ◆ ◆

I did it. It was me.

Me.

…But.

(A hundred years. A hundred years.)

◆ ◆ ◆

Atop a telephone pole. Just after nightfall.

I was standing on one leg like always, wobbling back and forth like a roly-poly toy for fun. The ultramarine sky of summer was incredibly expansive even at night. It threatened to suck you in. *Momoooo, still nothing?*

Tonight, we were in a refined, expensive residential area that unfolded near the mountains. There weren't too many people on the streets at night. The cicadas were singing, and

I could hear automobile engines in the distance. The houses were all magnificent and massive, lit up invitingly.

Momo finally appeared from around the corner.

Tch! I clicked my tongue. *She's got an older woman on her arm now, doesn't she? I told her younger's better. Well, whatever. We do this every day—I can't afford to be too fussy.*

I dropped down rapidly, the hem of my long skirt billowing out, my long hair fluttering up, a lion's mane in the wind. I alighted without a sound behind the two of them, holding my breath, keeping myself hidden. *And the game begins again.* I liked my prey the most at this moment, when they were focused on talking with Momo, unaware of the Bamboo behind them. Humans smiling, their guards down. Like idiots.

Her salt-and-pepper hair was permed. A dry neck poked out from a high-quality linen blouse. Her voice, though, was still younger than mine. But I guess it would be.

"Once you get to that house, turn at the second corner—oh! To the left. When you do that, there'll be a house that's been painted green, all right?" The older woman kindly gave Momo directions, Momo looking like she would burst into laughter at any second, nodding with a meek look on her face all the while.

I pushed my head between them, and Momo snorted, suppressing a laugh. She looked at me out of the corner of her eye, her smile deepening.

My prey finally cocked her head, curious at Momo's sudden silence, and looked over at the girl beside her. *Now, she'll notice this girl with no nose, no ear, and no arm, and she'll scream. Heh heh, this is fun! Another night hunting.*

She shrieked.

The instant she did, I tumbled through the air several times and landed on my back as if blown away by a sudden squall.

Stunned to her core, Momo turned around. My prey also stopped and looked down on me in surprise. "M-miss—er? Huh?" She began to look back and forth between me and Momo. My strange appearance. Momo and the unfathomable look rising up on her face. Sensing danger, her face stiffened. She retreated one step, then another.

A small dog popped its head out of the bag on her shoulder. *Bark bark! Bark! Bark!*

I started shaking.

"What?" my prey murmured.

Momo hurriedly reached out. She tried to grab the woman's neck, but Momo had never really done anything like that, and she lacked nerve. The woman pulled away from her. My prey staggered into a run, almost pitching forward onto the ground.

"S-someone! Excuse me! Someone! Help!" The woman tried to shout, but her voice betrayed her.

I put my right hand down on the ground and staggered to my feet. Even though I was long used to not having it, the lack of a left arm made it hard to get my balance back immediately, and I fell on my back. "Dammit," I muttered, as I kicked at the ground and flew up.

"Marika? She's getting away!"

"Ngh! Like I'd let her!" *She's supposed to be my prey. She's a human. How dare she!* I flew into a rage.

The dog kept barking.

Dog! A dog... Honestly! Don't worry about it. It's fine... Fly!

My prey rounded the corner and tottered out of sight.

I'll get you!

I could hear her wild breathing. *Haah! Haah! Haah!* The sound of the heart of a human getting the wrong idea—that I was some kind of killer—and panicking. Slowly but surely, this was starting to be fun again. It was plenty exciting. The nightly hunt! Old hat for me now.

The dog barked.

I descended abruptly, but I so spectacularly failed to stick the landing it was kind of amazing. I fell directly behind my prey like a piece of garbage flung onto the road. I might have been old, but this was over-the-top! Not at all Bamboo-like! *Hurry up! Jump one more time!* In a syncopated, staggering rhythm, my prey dropped her bag and let out a high-pitched scream before running, escaping.

I flew again. The shrill barking of the dog grew distant. My prey kept running. She jerked her chin up; it looked like she was struggling. I descended and perched on her shoulders, a large eagle. I had finally caught her!

Dig my heel into the back of her neck! I did it the way I always did, just enough so that she wouldn't die. At least, that's how it should have been. But.

Crack! I heard the sound of bones breaking.

Huh? I slowly got down from her shoulders. Floating horizontally, I stared at my prey's face in profile.

The middle-aged woman slumped to the ground. Her head hit the asphalt, face turned to one side. Eyes wide open. An expression of surprise was frozen on her features. Just as I wondered if her limbs weren't shaking slightly, the shuddering stopped.

Momo finally caught up with us. She bent over, breathing

hard, her hands on her thighs as she looked over at me. Sweat was pouring down her forehead, and the scholarly black frames of her glasses were also askew. She peered at my prey.

"For real, Marika?!" she cried out, in disbelief. "Come on! What about catch and release? This is supposed to be a game! Isn't it, Marika?!"

"It was the dog!" I roared.

"Huh? The dog? Why?"

"What was I supposed to do?!" *That's right! I mean, come on!* But on this trip with Momo, I had promised to take only blood, not lives. *But, like, Bamboo mess up sometimes!*

"Marika." Momo's voice was so quiet I almost couldn't hear her. "You killed someone, and you're asking me what you were supposed to do?"

"Sh-shut up!" I dragged the body away roughly and tossed it behind a tree in a children's park. In the distance, the dog was still barking. The dog… I wasn't going to listen to that thing anymore. I bit into the neck of the dead woman and furiously drank her blood. She wasn't young, but I wasn't in a position to complain.

The summer wind blew, and the scent of blood mixed in with it. The night turned dark red. When I was finally full and absently lifted my head, Momo was standing stock-still.

"Marika! Marika… What *is* this?" She was crying. Making *that* face.

Huh? Is she saying this is my *fault?*

I snapped. "It wasn't on purpose, okay!" I stood up, not wiping the blood away from my mouth. "Just forget about it! Come on, let's go!"

"But she was a nice person…"

"She was an old bag you didn't know," I said, surprised at her reaction.

Momo stared hard at me and said nothing.

For some reason, I brought up my right hand and slapped her. She burst into tears. I turned my back on her and bit my lip hard. She didn't seem like she was going to stop crying anytime soon. This was a problem. *Stop. I'm telling you, don't be difficult.*

I left the park and started walking. The night road. When I walked, even the air shook like it was boiling. The cicada song gradually returned to my ears. It was like the closer you were to the asphalt surface of the ground, the higher the temperature.

I looked back. Momo was still crying, but even so, she was following me. I was relieved. I floated up from the ground and tried flying. Slowly. And I looked back again. Right around the end of the residential area. The dark national highway.

Momo was still following me.

I spun around and came down lightly beside her. Her tears kept coming. But when I reached my arm around her slim waist, she didn't resist... What a relief. We'd made up once again. I flew into the air and struck a pose that made us look like a strange constellation in the night sky. Momo's sobbing suddenly got louder. I basically had no idea why she was crying and getting so sad over the fact that someone she didn't know had died. Momo was a weird kid, you know.

✦ ✦ ✦

A tunnel. An unbending white passageway from the subway station. Dead silent. Like no one else existed in this world.

Because I forgot to steal the woman's wallet, we were spending the night here today. The cold tiles were apparently comfortable; Momo slowly closed her eyes. Crouched up against me, her tears stopped, and I felt a weight lift from my chest.

Suddenly, just when I was thinking she was asleep, she asked, "Why did you get so freaked out when the dog barked?"

I opened my eyes. For some reason, Momo was watching me closely. Was she still thinking about that thing from before? I rolled my eyes. I wrapped my arm around her and looked away.

"A long time ago, I had a dog. I suddenly remembered. That's all!"

"You're a Bamboo, but you had a dog?"

"No, that's not it!"

"Huh? Then…is this when you were a human being? You never talk about that. What was the dog's name?"

A faint breeze blew through the tunnel, the wind lukewarm like tepid water. It was just us in there, so the tunnel was silent again. Momo still seemed sad, but nevertheless, she was apparently trying to bore a hole in my face with her eyes.

I sighed and opened my mouth. "Fal. Falstaff." I gave voice to the dog's name. For the first time in around a hundred years.

An avalanche of memories tumbled from the night sky…

I grew up in a nice residential neighborhood, like the place we were hunting tonight. Square three-story house. One older sister. She excelled at everything. I was just average. My father, a manager at a pharmaceutical company, was incredibly together, a man who hated dishonesty, who loved the straight and narrow. Given that his work involved selling pharmaceuticals wholesale, he should have been forced to toe the line with the mafia, but he always went head-to-head with them.

One day, he came home from somewhere with a dog. Said it was a present for me. This was a mixed blessing.

It was right before my younger brother was born, and I guess my parents thought I might hate him. So they decided to turn the focus of my attentions on a dog.

"This is your dog, Marika," my father said. "He's your responsibility. You've got to take good care of him."

So, reluctantly, I started taking the animal for walks, making sure it peed and stuff. And the puppy was stupid. I'd teach him things, and he'd forget all of it right away. Training him was super annoying. But he loved food and walks and playing. And he slept like the dead. I wasn't falling for him and loving him the way my parents had hoped, though.

But one day...

"One day?"

"You're still listening? I was going to stop. I thought you went to sleep. One day—so, like, I was almost kidnapped, okay?" The memory flickered back to life as I continued. An ancient Bamboo reminiscing about the old days—just remembering was an effort in and of itself...

The denizens of the underworld despised my father's strict management policies. So one day, when I went out to walk Fal, I was suddenly surrounded on all sides by black cars. And I thought, "Oh! This looks like the end!" I surrendered to my fate pretty easily. Because there wasn't anything I really wanted to do in life to begin with, you know? Unlike my father and my sister, I wasn't particularly smart or anything.

And then Fal, this supposedly stupid dog, started barking his head off and biting the men who closed in on us, nipping their ankles. So they kicked him, and he went flying like an old rag. I thought he was dead. I mean, he was a pretty small dog, kind of puny. But he sprang up and came running back over, barking half-crazedly the whole time.

One of the men pulled out a gun. He fired at Fal as the dog was racing around on the ground. Fortunately, he didn't hit him, but then Fal sunk his teeth into another ankle and stayed put there. So I knew the second shot would definitely hit him. I threw myself at the man with the gun. I never dreamed I had that kind of courage in me, you know? The bullet went off course and hit Fal right in the tail. He let out this earsplitting yelp as half his long brown tail went flying. And then he started barking even more, if that was possible, bleeding the whole while.

In all the commotion, I guess someone called the authorities to report what was going on. The police arrived, and the black cars all raced off in the blink of an eye. Fal had saved me.

After dealing with the police, we took Fal to an emergency vet and got his tail treated. He howled in pain. He was really suffering, and he bit my hand hard. And then he turned his little beady eyes up at me as if to say, "Sorry for biting you." I stroked his head. He whined pathetically.

That's when I really started doting on that dog. It was

like we had forged this bond or something. I went out of my way to give him delicious treats. I would brush him and tell him how much I loved him, my little darling. I hugged him, rubbed my cheek up against him, ran my hand down his back lovingly.

Eventually, my little brother was born…

"And then?"

The white tunnel, illuminated. The air a mix of summer heat and the cool from the day's air conditioners. It wasn't a popular spot; it was still just me and Momo.

I shrugged lightly. "Look, I told you before, didn't I? My family was killed too, just like yours. I said we had a lot in common that way, right? So, like, one night…when I went home…"

"Where were you coming home from?"

"Mm. Hmm." I nodded vaguely. "The minute I was there, standing in front of my house, I knew something was different somehow. But something else had happened that day too, so I thought maybe it was all in my head, like it was me that was different. But that wasn't it… There was a strange man in the entryway. A Bamboo. The mafia in that town hired Bamboo, too. My father, my mother, and my sister were lined up on the floor already. My little brother was hidden under the sofa. Wrapped in a blanket. Yeah, he was alive. The Bamboo hadn't noticed him. But he noticed me. I guess he was already full—he didn't drink all my blood when he attacked me. The police took me away, just another dead body, and then in the morgue of the police hospital—"

I woke up all alone in the middle of the night. Everything was cold, and the whole world looked different somehow. I jumped up in terror and slammed into the ceiling. I couldn't control my power then. I fled the hospital, killing a doctor along the way, so the police came after me. They shot at me, and several bullets hit me right in the chest. But I didn't die. I didn't have the first clue about what was going on, so I just hid for a while.

"And…ever since, all these years, I've been a Bamboo."

"What happened to your little brother? Did they rescue him? And what about your dog?"

I closed my eyes. I didn't get why Momo was worrying about a kid she didn't even know.

The tunnel was quiet, filled only with the echo of our voices. The place was deserted. And chilly, despite the summer, almost like the morgue that day.

"Marika…"

"Go to sleep, Momo!"

"Hmm."

I opened my eyes again. Momo was quiet, a pensive look on her face. I wondered what she was thinking about.

"Momo, tomorrow we're going to take the subway someplace far away. We have to get away from this town. I mean, it's gonna get pretty sketchy for us when they find that body!"

She said nothing.

"We haven't killed anyone before this, so we were safe. Those guys're up to some shady things too, you know?"

Still her mouth stayed tightly shut.

"Just go to sleep, Momo."

Momo's answer was so quiet I couldn't catch it. What was up with her?

✦ ✦ ✦

And then it was autumn. And Momo suddenly grew up.

"Come on, Momo. Let's go!"

"Hold on. Just a little longer."

"Huh? How long's a little?"

"I told you, I still need to talk to him, Marika." She spoke to me like she was admonishing a spoiled child, and I looked back in surprise.

A lukewarm breeze danced around me, tangled with the leaves of the trees, and made my black hair dance like a long tail. Then it set the left arm of my thin khaki coat fluttering. "About what?" I asked, my voice muffled on the other side of the mask that covered my nose and mouth.

Night was just starting to fall at the convenience store along the national highway running through a provincial city. Momo was standing in front of the magazine racks, talking to a boy in glasses. He had been there the day before too, at the same time. He looked my way with a kind smile, the photography magazine he had been reading still open in his hands.

I tugged fiercely on Momo's sleeve, and she looked at me with a sigh. "I said, wait!"

"It's just—we gotta get going."

"You're such a pest! God!"

I couldn't believe my ears. Impossible that Momo would talk to me like that. I slumped forward and stepped out of the store. With nothing in particular to do, I flitted around in the night sky until Momo finally came out. She waved amiably toward the inside of the store and then started walking briskly.

A small truck whooshed past on the highway.

Momo didn't want to move from town to town all the time anymore. Even though she knew it was dangerous, she wanted to stay in the same place for several days at a time. She'd turned into a grown-up, become obstinate. She wasn't as docile as she used to be.

Slowly spinning, I oriented my face so it was upside down relative to Momo and peered at her. "Get it together. Let's go to the next town already."

"Marika. I just—" she started to say, then stopped. But her feet didn't. She moved steadily forward, her face hard for some reason.

"Found tonight's prey!" I joked, still upside down.

"You look like a calligraphy brush when you fly like that, Marika. It's weird."

"Let's get that dumb guy from before. You know, the one you were talking to. Say something to lure him outside."

"What are you talking about? Honestly!" Momo's voice was ice.

I hid my anxiety and kept flying, grinning. Then I whirled around, turned myself right side up again, and started walking alongside her. We were god-of-death wannabes. The perfect pair. That's what we were supposed to be, right? *I gotta keep up with Momo and charge forward into the future!*

"Okay?"

"…No."

"Why not?"

"Because!" She sighed in obvious annoyance.

The wind blew. Dry and light, the brown leaves danced, shed by the roadside trees. They writhed like dying insects on the asphalt, stirred up by the wind. What on earth was her problem? It was like she just kept getting further and further away from me.

+ + +

(Already a hundred years since then. Unnh. I can't actually believe that much time's passed.)

+ + +

And how many days has it been already in this backwater dump?

I was pretty sick of this boring provincial town and was worried about being found out. It wasn't a big place, which meant outsiders stuck out in a pretty real way. And yet Momo was all low-key and laid-back. My patience was wearing seriously thin.

We were inside a closed, but large, coffee shop along the highway, the place we had made our headquarters. Totally dark and dusty. I was sitting on top of an old square arcade table with a video game built into it when Momo finally came back. *Where've you been wandering to, Momo? Honestly—huh?*

Someone came in behind her. It was that guy. Wearing his idiot glasses. The one reading the photography magazine.

Still sitting cross-legged on the table, I slowly floated up to sit in midair. My long hair swung eerily from side to side. I wasn't wearing a mask, so my shaved nose was in full view. The boy drew back in fear.

"What's going on, Momo?" I asked, my voice that of a wrinkled old woman.

"So, like, Marika?" Momo's was that of a bubbly young woman. "I need to talk to you, actually."

"Talk? Start with what he's doing here!"

Momo dropped her head, looking conflicted. And then she pulled her head up again. "Marika. I, like...I've decided to stay in this town," she said, almost as if she were making up her mind right then and there.

"Huh?"

"I told him all about me! And his family runs a photography studio. They're looking for someone to work in the office, and he says they'd hire me! He says everyone should settle down and have a job with responsibilities!"

"What?! Are you serious?!"

"I—! I don't want to travel aimlessly like this anymore. We've been doing this for a year, you know. I'm a year older. And I'm tired of it."

I can't even believe this! I was dumbfounded.

Momo and the boy exchanged looks.

In other words, she'd found someone new to protect her, so she was done with me. For a second, I didn't know what to think. My feelings about Momo and my feelings for myself sort of slammed up against each other. But the Momo ones lost pretty quick.

I'll take him from you! Dark flames shot through my body. Reaching my right arm up to the ceiling, I spun around at top speed, a juggernaut heading straight for them.

Now, a night of hunting! The thrill is everything! It's all old hat to me!

The boy fled behind the dusty counter, keeping Momo behind him. Old coffee cups and piles of plates crashed to the floor and shattered. I could hear Momo screaming. The wooden counter was brittle from years of wear. I whipped my right arm down as hard as I could to flatten it. I reached out to the boy, grabbed his thin neck, and pulled him up. Momo was yelling something. The boy was shouting, "Momo! Run!" But she turned around.

"Marika, what are you?! I don't even know!" Her eyes were wild.

I looked down on her coolly.

"Why do you go around attacking people? I'm sick of it! I mean, we do this terrible thing to these grown-ups, total strangers. I hate it. I've hated it for a while now. I've hated it so much I could hardly stand it! But I was scared that if I left you alone, you'd kill people again. I couldn't let you out of my sight. So I've been dragging myself along after you, all the way to this place... My hands are so dirty..."

"Huuuh?"

"Marika, please! Promise me you won't kill anyone anymore! For my sake. I just need you to promise, and then I can relax. I can stay in this town. I can finally grow up."

Anger and sadness surged up in my heart. And also exasperation at this happening now, after all this time. "I-it's just, I don't have any choice, do I?!" I shouted back. "I mean, I'm a Bamboo! I-I'm a monster!"

I turned toward the wall and slammed the boy into it. He bounced and came to a stop on the floor. A chair fell over with a clatter. A moment later, the coffee maker hit the ground, and the glass carafe broke.

From time to time, I heard the sound of a car racing along the highway outside.

Momo's eyes glittered, tears threatening to fall even now. I had absolutely no idea what was making her that sad. Seriously. Seriously. I honestly didn't get it.

"You're wrong, Marika. I mean, the first Bamboo who took me in, he worked a regular job. H-h-he…" she said, like she was squeezing it out, like it was painful. "He was a good person."

"What the hell?"

"I was a total stranger, and he saved my life. And he died for it."

"Huh?"

"So I—all this time, I felt like I wasn't *allowed* to be happy. But I had it backward—that's exactly why I *have* to be happy. I figured that out talking to this boy. I can't keep living this life. I have to actually live for real. For Mustah's sake. And for Kyo's. That way, their flames will always keep burning. Right, Marika? I mean, you know that, too. I'm your best friend. There was a time when you loved me, wasn't there?" Momo pleaded, still looking about to burst into tears. "Right?"

I glared at her. *I don't know! No idea what you're going on about, Momo! I'm telling you! For real! S-so—*

"I'll tell you then!" I roared. My hair practically stood on end, I was so angry.

I mean, the pathetic kid who had trailed after me that day, weeping sadly, nowhere else to go—she was gone now. That adorable, pitiful Momo had completely disappeared. At some point along the way, she had turned into a regular grown-up. She'd changed. Into this boring jerk. Unreal! We were too cool for this. We were gods of death! We had so much fun. *Did you forget all of that? Stupid Momo! Stupid!*

I drifted along, parallel to the floor, and then righted myself next to the boy lying on his side. I went around behind his head and brought my heel up. The usual way.

And Momo shrieked. She charged at me. So quick I was dumbfounded. *Are you Bamboo, too?* Slammed into me. Tangled together, we crashed into the dirty window. The glass broke, and the cool outside air poured over me. We tumbled to the floor, covered in shards that glittered like ice. Momo was at my back and had both hands wrapped around my throat, and she was not letting go. She absolutely would not let go. I bared my tapered teeth and howled for all I was worth. I shivered from the chill of the cold air.

"This! This! This!" Momo hit me. "I won't let you kill people anymore! Marika! I won't let you be a murderer! I mean, like, not a single person in this world deserves to be murdered. E-e-everyone—they're trying as hard as they can, just to make it through this life. I finally get that now. Uh-huh. I didn't understand it before. I thought human beings were dumb, worthless. Which is why—I can't travel with you anymore. I can't be with you for even one more night. This—!"

She's so weak.

"This! This!" she shouted, straddled over me lying on my back as she continued to whack me with her pathetic tiny fists.

"I won't let you do this!" I stared up at her. "I'm totally taking you with me, Momo! We've got forever ahead of us! You can't fight that. You got some nerve for a human!" I put a little effort into it and rolled across the floor so that I was on top of her now.

She stretched out her skinny arms and slapped my face,

still yelling. "You damned vampire! I hate you! You suck! Murderer! Pervert! You always have to take them down with a kick to the back of the neck with your heel, huh? And you always look like it's sooooo much fun! It's not just that you want blood—you actually love preying on people. Why, okay?! Why is that the only thing you do?!"

"I killed the dog."

"You pervert! Is it that much fun? A hundred years of kicking people in the back of the neck? Go to hell! Vampire! ...Wait, 'dog'?"

"I killed Fal," I said abruptly.

(It was me. I had done it. I still hadn't been punished for it.)

"...What are you talking about?"

Shaking, I got down off of Momo. I crouched on the floor. The boy staggered toward us, and Momo got up, coughing. They stared hard at me. I started speaking in a small voice.

My little brother was born. I was jealous. Fal did his usual playful frolicking, wagging the half a tail he had left, following me around. We were super close. Maybe I made him do it. Maybe he was just curious too. Fal went over to my brother's bed. I watched him and grinned. My brother started crying in terror. This happened three times.

My father called me in to see him. Because the third time, my brother got hurt. It was shortly after he'd been born. My mother wailed and screamed like she had lost her mind.

"It's your dog. Take responsibility and dispose of it." My father always got right to the point. I couldn't disobey him.

He didn't tell me to take the dog to the pound. He just left it to me. I couldn't go home with Fal.

That evening, thinking it was our usual walk, Fal was really excited, running and wagging his butt along with the half tail. We slipped through the expensive residential area, out to a field spreading out behind the neighborhood that he liked. I dreamed about how far I could run with him. That's what I really wanted. If only this childhood could last forever.

An hour passed, and the sun finally started to set. Before I'd gotten Fal, this was the time of day I'd have been playing with my friends in town. Once he was gone, I guessed I'd go back to that. If only this childhood could last forever. I stood stock-still. I saw my father's imposing face in my mind. Fal looked back, smiling. He realized I was crying and cocked his head to one side. But his mouth was still grinning happily. At that moment, I brought my heel up. A quiet cry slipped out of me. "Aah."

He looked up at me like he couldn't believe it. His noble eyes were clear, firm in the belief that the girl who was his super best friend would protect him forever, that nothing bad could ever happen when we were out walking, that he was safe. Those eyes.

The sun went down. I sat there for ages.

I dug a hole with my hands and buried Fal. My dog. The dog who had saved me that day. My dog, only mine.

I stood up slowly. And then I went back to my house.

✦ ✦ ✦

The minute I was there, standing in front of my house, I knew something was different somehow. I thought it was all in my head, that it was me that was different. But that wasn't it. The door was open, and a Bamboo was standing there. I smelled blood.

He attacked me, and when I woke up in the morgue...

"I was a Bamboo."

Which is why.

No one knows.

I still haven't been punished.

Even though it's been a hundred years.

"My little brother, an orphanage took him in. He grew up, he lived, he died."

"Marika..."

"Fal's long since turned to dust. He's nowhere in this world. My best friend. That little dog's gone now."

"Marika."

"I can't forget his face that time."

"So then you were doing that over and over again? Attacking when they were safe, kicking their necks to take them down. Stealing their blood and their money. Night after night," Momo said. "You have to stop it already! I feel bad for you, but I can't keep doing this."

"Momo—"

"Marika, I want you to stop attacking people."

"But I—! I think I've only got another ten years to live! At least stay with me till then. I promised I'd show you flowers blooming in the end, didn't I? Did you forget?"

"No, I'm telling you I can't—"

"That's not what you promised!" I clung to her, desperate like she had been that night. When had our positions been reversed? It was like I was the kid with no place to go now.

But Momo shook her head stubbornly. "It's time to say goodbye. I have to claim my own life."

How dare she?! Talking like a self-help book or something?!

"Momoooo! You big stupidhead!" I shouted. *No way. This is totally not how it's supposed to go.*

We glared at each other. And then Momo averted her eyes uneasily.

The sound of a car horn, then an engine, came from outside. No one said anything.

And then, from far away, trembling, the boy said, "Um."

"Shut up!" I scowled at him.

"Wah? Ah?" He jerked his head back.

"This is none of your business! This is all because you had to come along and butt in!"

"I'm sorry…"

Silence hung over us once more.

"Um, I…" Ever so timidly, the boy started to speak again. "Marika, I don't think it was your fault. Um! About what you said before. I mean, your father shouldn't have said that. You, like…you were just a kid."

I looked at the boy out of the corner of my eye and shook my head. "I'm the one who kicked him. It's my crime."

"But—"

"What?"

"I forgive you. If I were the dog, I'd forgive you."

"Huh?" I stared at the boy. "You're not the dog! You idiot!"

"I'm sorry… But." The boy cleared his throat. He lowered his eyes, momentarily confused. And then he lifted his face.

I said nothing. The boy and I stared at each other.

"I'd have…forgiven you…a long time ago."

The wind blew in through the missing window. After that, the boy, Momo, me—none of us said anything anymore. Like any further discussion was completely forbidden, something that didn't belong in this world.

Time flowed like cold water.

The sun came up. Time to say goodbye.

Momo stood slowly and then set up the blackout tent before gently guiding me inside it. I gripped her slender wrist and looked up at her.

"Marika, before…" She gently shook my hand off. "You were really going to kill him when you brought your heel up, weren't you?"

"What? …Not telling."

"She wouldn't have, Momo. Marika's not that kind of girl. I know it."

"I know Marika better than you do!"

"Momo—"

"I am the one! I know her better than anyone!"

"S-sorry…"

I couldn't say anything. I stared up at Momo, her back turned to me now. But suddenly I reached out for her pale legs from inside the tent.

"Momo! Don't go! Stay with me! I get it! He can stay with us too. It can be the three of us! Don't leave me. Don't leave me in a place like this. If I don't have you, I—" I squeezed it out: "I'll be so alone."

The words felt painfully real. One more time. "Alone…I won't be able to bear it…"

But I got nothing in reply.

Morning steadily drew closer. I heard their footsteps as they left. All alone, I went to sleep.

Night fell once more, and I woke up. Darkness filled the coffee shop. Momo was gone; no trace of her remained. I could tell from the air that she'd left me forever several hours earlier. I got out of the tent and stretched slowly.

Night. An autumn night.

I was again a Bamboo alone. Fifteen years old for a century already.

I couldn't really put it into words, but something seemed different from how it had been up until last night. When I stepped into the night and started walking, the heels of my boots ringing out, it wasn't my beloved Momo's voice that came back to life in my cold, empty Bamboo heart, but rather the voice of that stranger, the boy.

I'd forgive you.

(A lie. A lie.)

I'd have forgiven you a long time ago.

(Really? Really?)

I went outside and looked up at the night sky. The air was horribly cold, chilled. It was the start of winter.

I was seriously heartbroken.

Reaching my right arm out into the sky, I kicked at the ground and shot upward. *Night bird style!* The sky that night was vast and beautiful.

JASMINE

Asked for directions, I turned around in front of the large supermarket by the train station. As I did, the child holding my hand threatened to run off on her own to the opposite side of the street. "Whoa, now!" I hurriedly scolded her, loudly. "No running!"

The season was on the verge of passing from winter

to spring, into that warm, pleasant season. It was loud in the tumult of the change from evening to night. I passed groups of junior high students on bicycles, senior citizens apparently on their way back from a gathering. A housewife around my age pushing a stroller yawned when I passed her. In the distance, a crow cawed, followed by the honking of a car horn.

A map was thrust in front of me, and I peered at it. Right hand. The shape of the fingernails looked familiar. Small, round nails.

"Oh my!" I lifted my face. "It's you, isn't it, Marika?"

The skinny girl standing in front of me opened her eyes wide, shocked to the core. That face! I couldn't help bursting into laughter. She hadn't changed even a bit, not one bit, from the girl I remembered; it was almost surprising. The large blacks of her round eyes were wet, like she was crying, and the nose hidden under the mask was also exactly as it had been. The voluminous, long black hair danced in the warm breeze.

She wore a light-pink spring coat, and I was suddenly jealous of the adorable, dainty design, something which no longer suited me. The left sleeve fluttered and flapped.

Frightened, the girl took a step back.

"Right? It is you, Marika?" I said her name again. "Hey!" I grabbed her wrist with my free hand and felt her trembling. She jumped like she had been burned.

"What? Er, um. So you remember me, Momo?"

"Huh? What're you talking about? How could I forget? Don't be silly. But where have you been all this time? You've been a good girl, I hope? Oh! Or maybe all this time, I—"

I interrupted myself. "You knew I was living in this town? What? And you never came to see me?"

"You totally hated me, so…" Marika hung her head, embarrassed.

"What! Hmm. Oh, I guess I did." I suddenly remembered the fight we'd had when we parted and dropped my head, uncomfortable.

Silence.

Marika lifted her face ever so timidly. As she looked up at me, she started to smile again. Goodness, why did she seem so happy? She was still, always, a strange child.

"Anyway, Momo. You remembered me, huh?"

"Well, of course I did. But what's going on, out of the blue? I mean, it's been ten years, hasn't it? Maybe longer?"

"So, like, Momo?" Marika came in close, almost in a panic. "It's like, my time's up. I can tell. That day, I promised you, so I came back here. I wonder…if you remember? You know, the flowers? The flowers I told you I'd bloom? My final flowers. I think it'll be late tonight or tomorrow evening."

Flowers? Final flowers? What on earth was she talking about? As I cocked my head to one side in confusion, a distant memory flickered on the screen in the back of my mind.

I was sure I'd heard this story about flowers blooming. About how Bamboo lived for 120 years or so. And how in the end, they bloomed beautiful white flowers just like the tall grass.

Right, I had cried and begged her, *Stay with me forever, okay? But if you do leave me, then…at least show me those flowers, okay?* But that had been over ten years ago. Back then, I'd felt like this far-off future would never come.

But actually, the season for those flowers was around the corner. Just like that. The flow of time is quick like water, I suppose. A person's life—it's surprisingly short.

Marika slowly removed her mask, exposing her tragic face. The child ducked behind me, afraid. I patted her head to reassure her while I looked down at Marika. She really hadn't changed at all. It was almost frightening, you know?

Marika reached her right arm out like a ghost and wrapped it around my neck. She put some power into it, squeezing. I felt an instinctive terror. Right, Marika wasn't human. She was a sad monster who had lived 120 years as a little girl.

"M-Mari—"

"Heh heh." But she soon pulled away and flashed me a grin as if to hide how she clung to me. "You seem regular happy, huh, Momo? Like a textbook, you know?"

"I-I—Marika. You saved me... To this day, you're the only one who knows."

"I told you, enough of that. Okay? Come on, Momo!" Marika whirled around on one heel and started to run. Aah, just like always, she moved effortlessly, like an animal.

Dragging the child behind me by the hand, I hurriedly chased after her. I couldn't run like I used to anymore, though. I stomped along somehow.

The moon was coming out, like a ship putting out to sea. The darkness behind the supermarket. The fog gradually growing thicker.

It wasn't the fog of that early evening from back when I hunted with Marika; it was a cold fog, something not of this world. I heard a dog bark somewhere. I could see a vision of a puppy racing along behind Marika, wagging his stubby tail. What, a dog? What was that about again? I was sure I'd heard that story too. But it was a long time ago, at any rate, and I was so busy all the time now. *Huh? Marika? Where did you go?*

I reached the empty lot in the back. Marika turned around, grinning from ear to ear. The fog grew even thicker. It really wasn't of this world.

"So, okay, Momo?" Marika beamed, as she started to tell me something. Like she wanted to confess a secret she had kept for too long. "Like, I—"

But she abruptly fell silent, a look of surprise on her face. She took a breath and then opened her mouth to try to speak again, but it seemed that her moment had come sooner than she'd expected. She didn't have the time left to finish telling me, her old friend, what she had started to say.

"Marika?"

(Mo. Mo... So I... So I...)

"Marika?"

(Traveling. With you. That time. Was fun... I. Love...)

"Marika..."

The wind gusted up, and I lost sight of her.

And then, before I knew it, these tiny white flowers— flowers I'd never seen before—sprang up all around, blooming one after another in succession, so bright, so vivid that they dyed the night sky white. Until finally the blossoms fell to the ground and scattered, and the skinny figure of the little girl was no longer anywhere to be found. So this was the death of a Bamboo! A monster so strong, so frightening, and yet ultimately ephemeral.

"Marika!" I called out in a small voice.

But I heard nothing in reply. I would never know what she'd been trying to tell me in her final moments.

3.

YOU WILL GO
TO THE LAND OF
THE FUTURE

Back then, I had a little brother. A small one.

NIGHT

Since time immemorial, there had lived a community of mysterious creatures deep in the mountains—grass monsters with great life spans, who were active only at night and put nothing other than the blood of human beings and other animals into their mouths. They were called the *takezoku*— the bamboo tribe—and they had long been feared by the humans of the villages. No, not simply feared; the humans perhaps also held them in a curious kind of esteem. Because the takezoku—*we*—were orderly monsters. Not only did we raise livestock such as water buffalo and mountain goats for our own food, once we drank the blood of these animals, we shared the meat, organs, and flesh with the humans. We could also fly, and we were stronger than the humans of our size. So, for instance, if a large tree was about to fall on a bridge, one or two takezoku who happened to be in the area could easily catch it and save lives. Before we knew it, the humans revered us as "the protective gods of the mountains" and started offering ten young men and women to us at their annual harvest festivals.

Our magnificent castle and the houses of our people were spread out on the face of a mountain blanketed by beautiful bamboo forests, looking down on the cramped human settlements at the base. A darkness not of this world led the way even deeper into the mountains. The white plaster of the castle gates rose up against the cliff, the silver towers of the large main building shining beyond them. On the other side of the gates were neat rows of the square white houses of the common takezoku, the echoing cacophony of the Yellow River's upper streams flowing along behind them.

And in the castle?

In that old castle, which had been sitting there for who knew how long…

The great hall.

In the light of the moon, my eyes slid open. The usual start of the night. I stretched long and hard within my length of orange light-blocking fabric. I'd slept the entire day away, wrapped snugly in this blanket suspended from the ceiling on silver ropes at a height around that of a person. I jumped nimbly to the floor. Stretched again.

I looked around and saw any number of silver ropes snaking down from the ceiling of the hall like the silk of hell spiders, holding aloft the noble members of the royal family as they slept wrapped up in blackout drapes of red, yellow, green, purple, blue.

I was the royal family's fifth child. The third princess. Two older brothers, two older sisters. And one younger brother.

I had dropped down still naked, so I kicked lightly at the floor and flew up to take the orange cape in hand and fling it around me. I set on my head the hat covered in fine silver decorations that I kept inside the cape. The long, thin adornments were in the shape of bamboo stalks and were only permitted to the royal family; they clanged coldly against each other like ice in water.

The blue hammock next to me wriggled and squirmed, and then a naked boy of about twelve or thirteen rolled over with a lazy yawn and dropped to the ground. Such a simple movement, and yet he landed on his backside, almost comically.

"Morning, Sis!" He laughed with embarrassment when he noticed me looking down at him.

"You really know how to make an entrance, hmm, little idiot?"

"Huh? It's just—" Faced with my exasperation, the baby turned beet red and began squirming.

"What?"

"I mean, I'm a total loser!"

"Th-that's not true!" I said, flustered. Now I'd done it.

But my brother continued, innocently, "But, like, our brothers tell me every day that I'm a runt. They say I'm the most useless member of the royal family. Our sisters too."

"S-so, uh, this is just what I think, but…I feel like you being born with that small body, the way you never really grow, I mean, there must be some kind of meaning in that. We just don't know it yet. But when a door closes, a window opens, you know! And, I mean, you—you just gotta put your mind to it, and you can do anything!"

He said nothing in reply.

"What? What's with the weird face?"

"Either you sorta make sense or you're kinda weird. Sometimes, I really don't know."

Now I was silent.

"Maybe it's just that you're too smart? You do way better than our brothers in Father's governance classes."

"Mmm." I held my tongue. It was true my work in class wasn't bad, but I was still probably the oddball of the royal family.

Perhaps awakened by our conversation, the brightly colored light-blocking hammocks around us began to wriggle and twist, and soon our brothers and sisters dropped down to the floor one after the other. Their pale, symmetrical nudity on display, they stretched in unison. They were quite tall, with almond eyes that suited their faces and proud noses. Magnificently attractive in both face and form, they made it easy to see why the humans held us in reverence as the gods of the mountains.

I, however, was smaller in stature, and if pressed, I'd say my face was more on the average side of things. And my youngest brother was sickly and also rather average looking. On top of that, he had stopped maturing when he was still a child. The two youngest members of the royal family were noticeably different from the rest.

"What's this?" Our eldest brother looked down on us, truly annoyed. "You little runts are up too early for no reason at all."

"Good morning, Brother!" my little brother replied breezily. Unlike me, he had always been an easygoing child.

"Heeey, early birds with no worm to catch!" our second brother muttered, sounding still drowsy as he wrapped his dazzling naked body in light-blocking fabric. "Go check on things outside the gates before Father's lesson! And…" He hung his head. His voice steadily grew thinner, anxious. "Tell us how things are outside."

Although my eldest brother was working to make it seem like everything was fine, this brother, urged on by our sisters, was worried. He furrowed his shapely brow.

Outside the castle, I let my gaze drift in the direction of the gates. "That commotion *has* been going on for a while now, huh?"

"Right?"

"Ohh, so then—" I started to say.

"Whatever!" My eldest brother cut me off. "Just go look!"

"I mean, you're smart and fast, right?" My second brother got serious and argued further, "*And* you have lowborn friends outside the castle. Right?"

"Mmm." I wasn't sure about going out before class. I stared up at my second brother.

My baby brother latched on to me, needy, a spoiled child. "I want to meet your friends! Please! Take me outside!"

I ended up nodding with a wry smile. He might have the appearance and heart of a child, but he had always excelled at keeping the peace. And he knew I was particularly susceptible to this sort of pleading. Plus, I was also curious about what was happening outside the gates.

We walked out into the hallway, our backs turned to our brothers and sisters, and I pulled on my little brother's hand. We flew through the castle, beyond the walls, outside. My brother's hand in mine had the pudgy feel characteristic of a child, but he was takezoku, so it was the chill temperature of ice, which made it even more beloved to me.

The moon was excessively bright. The light of the early

night. The stars also glittered and shone. The winter was not yet over; a light smattering of snow danced down. Illuminated by the moonlight, the flakes looked like fragments of stars.

"Aaah, it's so pretty!" My brother looked up in delight.

"It is." I nodded, and then I shot up into the night sky. As if to drop down on the other side of the stars.

I was a takezoku by birth! And a daughter of the royal family! So the night was an inexpressibly delightful time.

◆◆◆

We moved away from the castle and danced up into ever-higher reaches of the sky, wrapped in silver light, black hair and blackout capes fluttering in the wind, the ornaments on our hats jangling and clanging. Despite the brutal cold, the one layer of fabric was more than enough. The wind nipped and pulled at my cape to flash pale arms and legs, stomach and back, and occasionally the skin of my chest.

I circled the castle lightly three times, and once my body grew accustomed to the wind, I headed for the gates and the white walls that were dug into the face of the mountain and that surrounded the castle. Soon I smelled fire, and then a sea of torches came into view. This was what my second brother had ordered me to check on.

For the last month or so, things had been strange in the village at the foot of the mountain. Young people were moving in, and they looked different in both face and dress from the villagers who had lived there since olden times. Before we knew it, these newcomers had exploded in number. And they had no reverence for the takezoku, the gods of the mountains.

Yes, the young people had started to gather around the castle gates, trickling in one by one, bearing torches, to keep watch on the takezoku. The height of rudeness! We would never hurt humans! Naturally, it did happen that a newly born, inexperienced takezoku would occasionally attack someone, but the majority of us lived amicably alongside humanity. Was there ever a tribe of monsters so peaceful? Which was why I was baffled as to what this fuss was all about.

My brother clung to me, frightened, causing me to lose my balance and spin around. Right, this was the first time he was seeing this.

Torches in hand, the young people looked up at us and howled in terror. Some were inexplicably angry. The commotion grew.

What? Was a person flying this unusual?

They opened their mouths, dumbfounded, pointing fingers, yelping and shouting. I caught the eyes of a young woman in the very back who was about as old as I still looked. She stared at me with terror and confusion on her face.

Ah! Some people were throwing stones! They fell heavily back to earth without so much as grazing me. Ridiculous.

I breezed past the gates like a large bird and set my sights on the Yellow River. I was silver cutting through the sky.

✦ ✦ ✦

"I'm opening up now. Just hold on… What? Your brother's with you too?"

My old friend's voice was accompanied by the sound of heavy feet. I could hear my friend running around frantically, picking things up inside. This went on for what I thought was a long time before, finally, the rough wooden door was pulled open.

There was a small round hole in the door, and my brother informed us that, given his small stature, he could surely slip through. He then demonstrated that he could and laughed.

It was the custom of the takezoku to have nobler houses further inland on the mountain, which meant that here, close to the river, was where the takezoku of low birth gathered. The small square house stank of livestock, but I liked coming to this area anyway.

We stepped in through the front door. The floor inside was made of the same earth as outside. Several people were still asleep, tucked away in blackout fabric suspended by old, frayed ropes stretching down from the ceiling. My friend welcomed us with a vessel of water buffalo blood taken that very night. Fresh and delicious. My brother was surprised, but he quickly gave his thanks politely and began to lap it up in a refined manner.

The back door led to the river and was set up so that you could come and go on a small boat. They had a large ship they were building, almost overly enthusiastically, anchored on the shore. And it appeared to be very nearly finished. When I asked what on earth it was for, I was told, "It's just a pleasure boat! Although this one lets you go a little farther to have your fun."

Thinking this suspicious, I stared at the ship.

"But what on earth is going on?" my friend said loudly, as if to distract me. "I mean, you never come over this early!"

"Oh, my second brother's such a worrywart. He's afraid of the situation outside, so he told me to go take a look. He won't go himself, you know."

"Ha ha! I guess you are always prowling around like this, though." My friend suddenly lowered his voice. "Oh, outside. You mean not us, but those people, yeah? So like, that, we're also, like you lot…"

Perhaps awakened by the sounds of our conversation, young men and woman began to drop down from the hammocks above us. Their slender naked bodies were exposed in the faint light of the oil lamp for a moment before they quickly pulled capes around themselves. They set shining hats on their heads before joining the seated circle one after another.

As they passed around a chipped vessel filled to the brim with water buffalo blood, they scrambled to be the first to share their own opinions and thoughts.

"It's been a month already. And the outlanders just keep on coming, right?"

"They're not villagers. They don't look like farmers."

"One of them gave me this red book. It's poetry. At first, they didn't see the takezoku as enemies, you know? And this girl said it'd be bad for her to have a book of poetry, so she gave it to me. She told me so many stories. It was fun. She said she was a university student from Beijing."

"Beijing? University? What's that?" I asked.

"At any rate, they're not like the people who've always lived on the mountain. They think differently, they act differently. And they really don't trust the takezoku. So they're out there like that, every night."

"It's like they're keeping watch on us," another said.

"So, like, I heard they have a plan to attack us," my friend said. "Well, I mean, we're the stronger ones, though. I wonder what they're going to do."

"They threw rocks at me before."

"Ah ha ha! Even though you're stronger than some rock!"

"But it's gotten harder to live on this mountain, you know?"

"Mm."

"Yeah."

And they gradually fell quiet. The sounds of breathing and fabric rustling echoed inside the hut. It was a strange silence. Like it was hiding something.

The burbling of the river was refreshing. I sighed along with it and brought the vessel to my lips when it came around to me again. Passed it to my brother. He had a strange look on his face as he glanced around at the assembled lowborn youths, but then perhaps understanding something in the silence, he began to ask questions about how to raise and prepare water buffalo. His innocent voice, free of any ill will, eased the tension in the room, and everyone started enthusiastically explaining the ins and outs of raising livestock.

Outside, the current of the river abruptly quickened and slackened over and over. Each time, the half-built boat rocked back and forth and thumped against the bank.

"Still, it's a large boat, hmm?" I looked back as we were about to leave. "Big enough for livestock even."

"Ha ha ha! The animals'd run around too much! And they're probably too big anyway! I mean, it's just a pleasure craft."

Even as he laughed, my friend averted his eyes seemingly

apologetically for some reason. What on earth was that about? Then the boat made another large clunking noise.

✦ ✦ ✦

The road home.

I flew past the castle gates once more. There were slightly fewer humans with torches. Some had grown tired and had settled themselves on the ground.

"But, you know, it's scary, Sis," my younger brother said, looking down on them. "'Cause we don't know why they're out here like this."

"Mm."

"I wonder why they hate us? I mean, we haven't done anything wrong."

"Where there is knowledge, there is not fear!" I said.

"Huh?"

"That means if we knew who those people were and what they were thinking, they wouldn't be scary anymore."

"Oh. Honestly, Sis, talking fancy again... What're we gonna do?"

"I think we should ask Father. I mean, he knows more than we do."

"What?!" My brother was surprised. "Father is so scary!"

"He is not! He might be imposing, but he's a person of reason. Which is exactly why he's able to rule the takezoku. His governance classes are also fascinating. If we ask him, he should answer us."

"You go ahead then." He clung to me tightly. And his tiny body was shaking! Was he really so afraid of Father?

"Yup! C'mon, tardiness is strictly forbidden! We have to get to class!"

"Ugh! You're so serious. I mean, you could skip out sometimes like our sisters, you know."

"Hey! What did you just say?"

"N-nothing!"

Grinning at each other, we descended rapidly, flaring into a ball of frozen orange and blue flame, and charged into the castle hall. Everyone else had already left, and the countless silver ropes dangling from the ceiling twisted and shook in the wind we blew up.

We made our way down the twisting and winding hallways to a small room deep in the castle where our father taught us governance. The air was silent and chilled. Countless flames flickered in countless candlestands attached to the walls, each one a different shape. The candles were all different sizes and colors, too. Red flames greeted us.

We took the seats at the very back among the low floor desks arranged in the room. Soon enough, our brothers and sisters came flying in from the hallway, laughing and chatting. They settled in gracefully at their desks in front of us and then stopped moving entirely, as if they were posing for a painting.

The candles flickered slightly. No doubt this was how it had been since time immemorial, the children of the royal family coming together in this way. Snowflakes wandered in on the night wind that blew in from outside.

And then my second brother looked back, his neck practically creaking, and raised his eyebrows. *So? How was it outside?* I started to answer—*So, all right*—when the magnificent door, featuring a depiction of a bamboo grove awash in moonlight, opened without a sound, and in came our father. I hurriedly closed my mouth. The six children of the royal family fell prostrate as one and welcomed the king.

"Now, then." My forehead firmly pressed against the floor, I heard my father's low voice above me. A sonorous voice with no hint of emotion. This was the voice of a king! "We'll begin tonight's lesson!"

I slowly lifted my head, unconsciously trembling. The children of the royal family each took a writing brush in hand. I looked up at the king with quiet admiration and fear.

Because the takezoku did not visibly age, at first glance he appeared to be the same age as his children. He was even slightly shorter than my older brothers. Thick eyebrows, large eyes and nose. He was wrapped in the heavy silver fabric that was the mark of the king, and standing on one leg, he slowly lowered himself to the ground, with one knee raised. The eyes he turned on us were cold and solemn. He had that particularly frightening look of someone who had borne a heavy responsibility for many years, a face which permitted absolutely no emotion.

But before he became king, he was a regular little boy. Cheerful, thoughtful, you know? I'd heard the takezoku commoners say with long sighs, but I couldn't believe it. The aura of intensity hanging around my father was simply too much that of a king.

Now then, the lesson. Again tonight, it was long and abstruse. My older sisters were quick to grumble, forthright in admitting they didn't understand a thing. My older brothers tried their hardest, but halfway through, they got lost. I was the only one who managed to somehow grasp the theory and ask what were apparently appropriate questions. While also helping my little brother next to me with quiet hints and explanations.

When the lesson was finally over, everyone let out exhalations of relief. And then my father began to call my older brothers and sisters before him one by one.

He turned first to my eldest brother. "You are the one who will inherit my place," he announced, his voice low and serious. "This means you will be the next king. All of this will be on your shoulders. Be strong!"

My eldest brother's face shone. "Yes, Father!" he replied, proudly.

"Dismissed!"

"Yes, sir!"

My second brother, then my sisters followed, and then finally child number five was called up. Me. My heart was filled with both anticipation and anxiety as I wondered what on earth he would say to me. I timidly lifted my head to see him looking down on me with unexpectedly severe eyes for some reason.

"You."

"Y-yes…"

"You *are* a very smart child. Which is why you must support your eldest brother. He will be king and may need it."

Aah, he'd complimented me! I was delighted. "Yes, Father!" I said, my eyes sparkling, like my eldest brother's had earlier.

"But when he does not need it, you must not raise your head!"

"What?"

"Knowing one's place is also a kind of intelligence!"

"Y…y-y-yes, sir…"

"Dismissed!"

Prostrated deeply before him, I forced myself not to cry and then stood and stepped back. I felt like the others were staring at me after witnessing this, grinning at me getting carried away just because I had some brains in my head. I was embarrassed. Was I an arrogant little sister? I could hear my older sisters whispering to each other *What did that mean just now? Huh? It's too difficult, I don't know.* I heard my little brother being called upon and was surprised. Even the little one was getting a warning today.

Dejected, I returned to my seat. The flames of the candles flickered two, three times in the wind, and it felt like the air in the room shook.

✦ ✦ ✦

"Outside? I see." Father nodded slowly. "So you lot are concerned as well."

Even though I'd just been told not to butt in, I couldn't stop the question from slipping out of my mouth. But my second brother praised me with his eyes—*Nice work, little sister. Thanks for asking*—so I looked up at Father expectantly. My eldest brother feigned ignorance of the whole affair. And my sisters just exchanged uneasy glances.

Father looked around at his children briefly. "I've been thinking quite a lot about that situation. I've had meeting after meeting with my ministers. Now I suppose you're *all* frightened, then?"

"Those people? They're not the least bit frightening!" my second brother countered, and then looked around help-lessly at our older brother and sisters.

"This is because of the Cultural Revolution." A cold smile rose up on Father's lips.

"Huh? The Cultural Revolution?" I blurted. My little brother next to me shuddered.

Father turned to me and slowly nodded before turning back to my eldest brother. "The Chinese government has changed. Academics and students from the cities are being sent to farming villages. The humans filling up the village at the foot of the mountain are some of these, apparently. The human government never ceases to interfere with us!"

"Oh, so then…" I remembered what one of my friends had said before about the book from the Beijing university student and nodded in understanding.

"What we should fear is their nature." Father narrowed his eyes suddenly. "Unlike the simple villagers who've been here since olden times, these ones, when they learn of the takezoku, only feel mistrust toward us. They have not a drop of reverence. They shun us, saying we are 'premodern relics' that must not exist!"

"B-but—" My eldest sister leaned forward. "They'll surely be gone soon! Th-the mountain will be peaceful for us once again. Our beloved, wonderful mountain life!" she said in a shrill, nervous voice, like she was praying for it to be true. My eldest brother nodded in agreement—*Right, of course it will.*

Our father's face grew stern, and he shook his head. "One who would be king must not embrace baseless optimism," he intoned, solemnly. "I teach you that every night! First of all, according to one theory, it will likely be quite some time before they return to their cities."

My eldest brother held his tongue.

"But then, Father. What are we to…?" my second sister asked tearily, pressing her hands together.

Father furrowed his brow. "We must assume the situation will continue and consider how we will respond."

"Respond?" Once more, I was unconsciously leaning forward. When he turned piercing eyes on me, I thought, *Ah, I've done it now. I butted in again.* I hurried to prostrate myself once more. I sensed a wry smile from my father, so I looked up timidly, and he ordered me with the palm of his hand to sit up, it was fine. With relief, I took up my previous posture. But I clamped my mouth shut tightly so I wouldn't make any more noise.

"Actually, you see." Father looked at the faces of his children. "There's a proposal to move. Deeper into the mountains. Into the darkness."

"What?"

"This site was originally selected, as it was fairly deep in the mountains. I suppose it can't be helped."

"Father, you mean…?"

"Into the mountains! In the darkness still untouched by human hands, we will build a new castle, rebuild our houses, add to our livestock, and create a new settlement! The number of humans carrying torches only increases each night. This is the era we live in! These are the days we see ahead now. However, we must not be too hasty. We'll likely make the announcement in a few days."

"S-so suddenly?"

My older brothers and sisters looked at each other, baffled. The flames of the candles shimmered. I could read nothing on my father's face. His silver crown glittered above it.

Into the mountains? Move deeper? The takezoku?

"And that is why," my father said, rebuking my eldest brother once again, "you must be strong. Stronger than anyone else."

My eldest brother's face stiffened, and he nodded. A little of the youth that had been there until moments ago disappeared, and his face suddenly seemed grown-up, as though he had awakened to his responsibility.

The flames of the candles flickered again.

◆ ◆ ◆

"About your friends."

"Y-yes?"

Our father stopped me after we'd flown out into the hallway and were about to go back to our rooms. I dropped awkwardly to the floor, ending up on all fours. Embarrassed, I stood up, my cheeks red.

"Friends? Um, oh! By the river? Oh! Yes. I just went and looked in on them earlier."

"They built a boat, yes?"

I recalled the boat and nodded. Yes, a rather magnificent ship for a pleasure craft. One that looked like it could hold plenty of livestock. What on earth was it?

Father suddenly grinned. A grin followed by a flash of something very unkingly and strangely boyish. "It seems some of the commoners are beginning to see that the takezoku will move into the mountains. Some among them are thinking of other routes."

"Other routes?" I looked up at my father and cried out, "Oh!" The king of the takezoku was examining the idea of moving the tribe into the mountains. And young people were building a boat at the same time for some reason. What if...

Father took on his very kingly stern expression again. "In meetings with my ministers, another idea was proposed. Besides climbing up into the mountains," he said, in a solemn, quiet voice.

"Another idea?"

"We could go down the river and out to sea, go to a different land, a different country. Personally, I don't think it's a bad idea, but most ministers were against it. And it doesn't seem too practical to emigrate when there are so many of us. I made an executive decision as king and rejected the proposal."

"...I see."

"However, if some enterprising citizens were to come up with the same idea and start building a boat on their own, that would be very interesting."

"What?" I was stunned. "So then you're saying you won't stop them? You won't punish them? I mean, they might be building a secret ship to go down the mountain on their own, to emigrate. Father? Of all people, I should think you, our fearsome king... You can't possibly! Oh! E-excuse me! I just—" The words had just slipped out.

But strangely, instead of getting angry, Father simply grinned once more. When we talked alone just the two of us like this, I felt like I could almost see how he had been a thoroughly ordinary cheerful youth before he became king. No, perhaps it was just my imagination. This great man was our king, after all.

"Of course, as the one who rules the takezoku, I must put a stop to any independent action like that... Which is why, you see, I've decided to not have noticed, officially."

"Huh? Umm..."

"The truth of it is, splitting our people into two groups slightly increases the probability of the takezoku's survival, of not being wiped out. In which case, it might be that I shouldn't stop them. No, that means..."

Bewildered, I looked up at him. Before he left, I thought I heard him mutter, "After all, even a king is uncertain at times." But I couldn't have. Our imposing, powerful, emotionless king would never let slip something so fainthearted.

♦ ♦ ♦

"Ah! You're back? What's wrong?"

Around dawn of that night, one of my friends called out to me suddenly from below, and I grew flustered. I spun round and round again in the silver sky, and then, my light-blocking cape fluttering lightly, I slowly descended and landed gently on the deck of the nearly complete ship stationed on the river.

A few more friends came out from the hatch and grimaced at each other upon finding me there. The babbling of the flowing water soothed me. The snow had only just stopped falling, so the deck was slick with moisture, shining transparently. Hesitantly looking at each of my friends in turn, I slowly cocked my head to one side.

✦ ✦ ✦

"That's right. We didn't build it to go sailing on the river. This is—we're planning to use this ship to leave the country. Yup!"

Invited once more into the rough hut, I sat cross-legged on the ground. I looked at my friends out of the corner of my eye as they busily finished up work on the ship and packed their things. "So that's it."

"I can't believe you figured it out. Oh! Right, so you went back to the castle and heard the idea about the takezoku moving into the mountains, and it just came together for you like that?"

"Uh? Y-yeah," I assented, vaguely. I couldn't just broadcast the fact that Father had been the one to realize what the boat was for.

Smiles grew on my friends' faces. Fortunately, it seemed that they had wanted to talk to me about this too. They took a break from the work and began speaking all at once.

"I mean, it's not like we were hiding it because we wanted to!"

"It's just, you're part of the royal family. We'd only be making trouble for you. You're so serious, you know? And…"

"We actually wanted to ask you all kinds of questions. You're so smart and everything."

"Like, those new people in the village down there, they have it in for us. And then we heard this rumor about moving deeper into the mountains. And, like, we talked about it every night. It's true that by going deeper the humans wouldn't find us, we'd be safe. But, like…"

"Basically, it'd be like deliberately running away to the past, you know? Right?"

"And we're young and all. We don't have property or status or anything. We live this broke life. So then, you know…"

"We thought about the opposite. The opposite of the mountains! Down the river, out to sea! Right? So then…"

A handsome young man in a corner of the hut who had been flipping through the poetry collection with the bright-red cover looked up. He picked up the thread in a quiet voice. "If the times are changing, then we have to go not to the past, but to a new world—the land of the future. Maybe that's our destiny."

"The land of the future?" I repeated in a small voice. The words almost shone with light, surprising me.

The young man nodded. I looked around, and the faces of my young friends seemed to be filled with a quiet hope. My heart pounded.

"Oh!" A different, larger youth approached, looking serious. "This was my idea, wasn't it?"

"Was it?"

"Now, look! I'm originally Japanese, right? I was traveling through this area, and the people in the village at the foot of the mountain tricked me. They made me a sacrifice for the harvest festival! But the old king thought I was interesting because I knew about this faraway country, so he saved me, transformed me into a takezoku! I was talking about that country on the other side of the ocean, and that's why you guys all started talking about going to check it out, instead of being scared about the whole idea."

"Oh, that's right. I totally forgot."

"Come on, you guys!"

"Well, anyway…"

I lent my ear to my friends' conversation, and the dawn grew closer bit by bit. I smiled, listening quietly.

"Basically, we're going to cross the ocean and look for new land. As long as night comes and we can raise livestock, monsters like us should be able to live happy lives pretty much anywhere! As long as we have courage in our hearts!" I heard a cheerful voice exclaim, and I nodded.

The sky outside was bright with pale light. If I wrapped myself very tightly in my blackout cape, I'd still be able to make it back to the castle. The whole point of each of us being given a cloth like this was so that we could go out during the day, after all. Aah, but…

"Hey, can I sleep here? So much is happening, and I'm learning all this stuff all of a sudden. I have so much to think about. And I'm totally exhausted by it."

"What are you talking about?! A member of the royal family sleeping in a filthy place like this?"

Rubbing my eyes, I turned around. A girl with short hair had opened her eyes wide in surprise. She hadn't said much of anything up to that point, maybe because she didn't quite get along with everyone.

"Why not?" I wrapped myself in my fabric and dangled from the straw ropes hanging down from the ceiling. "It's all the same to me."

"What? Really?"

"What?"

"Maybe I misjudged you…"

"Huh?" I closed my eyes and fell asleep, my head spinning in a million different directions.

✦ ✦ ✦

The next evening.

I stared blankly when I woke up, not knowing where I was. But then I remembered and grinned as I dropped down lightly.

My friends' hut alongside the river. The earthen floor was cool, damp, soft. Just like when I woke up in the hall at the castle, I assumed I was the first awake tonight, so given that I had a little extra time, I decided to take a look around. But two or three others were already awake, drinking blood from a vessel, packing up, going about their work.

"So, um," I said in a small voice, winding the orange light-blocking fabric around me.

"Hello. Wait, you slept here too? I didn't even notice at all!"

"Yeah. So I was thinking while I slept—um, no, wait. It's nothing." I shook my head.

The boy reading the poetry collection lifted his head and looked up at me curiously. A girl sitting near me pushed the vessel of partially drunk blood at me. I thanked her and took a big gulp. It was warm, filling.

The night became quiet again. My friends woke one after the other and naturally split off into groups to attend to the livestock, work on the boat, or clean the house. It seemed that there was no one person who might have been called the leader of the house.

I remembered the things they had told my little brother the previous night and quickly moved to help with the livestock, surprising the others.

"You're good at this! You really can do anything, huh?" one friend said.

I became embarrassed, wondering if I was in fact intruding again, and stopped what I was doing.

"You're good at this? Then help me," a different girl said, and handed me a tool. Quietly, matter-of-factly, each person became immersed in their work.

After working for a while, I muttered again to no one in particular, "I was thinking…"

One of my friends looked up. "Wait," she said, as if just realizing something. "Don't you have to get home at some point? Isn't it time for your governance lesson?"

"Yeah. It is. Um…"

"So what, then? That's quite a serious look on your face."

At this, the twenty or so people in the hut all stopped moving and looked toward me uneasily from wherever they stood.

I couldn't back down now. I slowly opened my mouth, mustered my courage somehow. "Uh, um…"

"What is it?"

"Can I come to the land of the future too?" My small voice echoed through the hut. My friends looked at me, expressions of surprise rising up onto their faces.

"You cannot!" someone shouted. Everyone else began to shake their heads in agreement. I looked around at them all, surprised.

The thoughtful-looking young man with the red poetry

collection stood up. On behalf of everyone else there, he spoke. "It's just...you're royalty. You're not like us. You're a girl of noble birth, aren't you?"

"But! I! It's not like I wanted to be born into royalty!" Even I was surprised at the words I shouted. And then I realized that I'd actually felt like this for a long time. I sent up a silent apology to my father and my siblings. In the next instant, my opposition to the royal family, the way it placed value on only the eldest boy, exploded. But then I remembered my father's face in profile, his expression almost that of an orderinary boy as he talked about the boat to cross the ocean, and love and respect filled my heart. I was confused. Suddenly, tears were pouring down my cheeks.

"You can't cry about it." The poetry boy slowly shook his head. "You're a noble person by birth. Er, so basically, it's common takezoku like us who can jump on this boat and go off into the unknown. Or, you know, guys like him who were born human and later became takezoku. You're just too wonderful for this."

Right, that's right. Everyone came together, timidly trying to convince me. A friend I was particularly close to touched my shoulder as if to comfort me. "The highborn are the backbone of the takezoku. You have to go into the mountains."

I guess so... My head hanging, I started to agree.

"Wouldn't that be good, though?" came a small sharp voice from a corner of the room, sounding annoyed. "If she came with us!"

Everyone looked back with a gasp. A girl with short hair was squatting on the ground, needlework in one hand. I remembered her from the brief conversation we'd had about me staying over before we'd gone to sleep that morning. She stared up at us, her face slightly dirty.

"Huh? What's with you all of a sudden?"

"I mean! This girl, she's supposedly smart, and she seems all right. You get to like her! I thought she was just faking it 'cause she's a royal. I've hated her this whole time. But then this morning, when I saw her just sleeping all fine like that, I realized I totally got her wrong. I'm fine with getting on a boat with this girl. She doesn't throw her weight around like the other princes and princesses. We'd prob'ly get along, actually. First of all—huh? Umm…" The girl had been speaking forcefully but then suddenly began to stammer and mumble, perhaps picking up on the still-unfavorable mood in the hut.

"Look!" she said earnestly, jerking her chin up. "There's that! We're, like, going really far away, and in the end, we're going as takezoku, so, you know…if we had a royal with us, maybe it'd give us a little courage. You know?"

"Courage, huh?"

"Right? Look, I mean, there's like a toy throne on the boat, so how about if there was maybe a monarch just for us, a royal kid? But a nice one!"

"H-huh? A monarch?" I parroted back in confusion. At most, I wanted them to let me on the boat as a nameless emigrant, but the conversation shifted abruptly to the liege of the settlers.

My friends looked at each other, glanced at me, and started discussing it all at once.

"Hmm?"

"Right!"

"Nah, we do like you and all."

"I mean, you're a princess, but you never look down on us."

"But, like, I heard she's the smartest and brightest of all six of the kids in the royal family. We can't take a princess this amazing and ask her to come be our king."

The boy with the poetry collection cocked his head to one side and looked around like he was considering the idea. Then he stared at me, examining my face closely.

It was time for my lesson; I had to go home. I moved to leave the hut, while the discussion continued, and put a hand on the old wooden door. I looked down on the small round hole in it and grinned, remembering my tiny brother joking that he could come and go through it as he pleased.

I looked back quietly as I pulled the door open and saw that the poetry boy had walked over to the girl with the short hair. They looked close; they pressed their foreheads together as they talked. The girl seemed to be passionately relating her thoughts, while the boy listened with a serious look on his face. I shot up and out into the night sky. The end of winter was at hand. Orange blackout cape fluttering behind me, I flew.

✦ ✦ ✦

On the way home, I thought I heard a shout from the world below. Looking closely, I saw a human girl on the ground face-down, her leg pinned under a fallen tree. Given what a bother it was, I wavered between abandoning her and helping her before dancing down and hoisting the tree up. And then the girl looked up at me and screamed.

I'd seen her face before. It was the young girl who'd been at the very back of the group with the torches. She crawled along the ground, screaming, trying to get away from me.

I was perplexed by her reaction, so different from that of the villagers accustomed to the presence of the takezoku. "You don't have to be so afraid. Did I do anything to you?"

The girl looked back at me holding the fallen tree up lightly and swallowed hard. "I-I'm...sorry!"

"If you would only learn about the takezoku." I lowered the tree to the ground. "Hey, meeting like this is a good chance and all."

"No! I don't want to...know anything!"

"What? Why?"

"I mean...I won't...I'll be different from everyone else!" The girl looked back and stared at me as if lost for a moment. And then she hurriedly began crawling away again. I simply stayed silent and watched her go.

I danced up into the night sky again. The air of the winter night was clear and chilly, like particles of ice had been scattered across the bowl of the sky. I flew intently forward, silent. Past the castle gates illuminated by the torches of the humans, to the castle.

Tonight again, flakes of snow floated to the ground, glittering.

✦ ✦ ✦

Back in the castle, the night felt very quiet. I hurried down the hallway, where flames of various sizes flickered at the top of equally varied candles, toward the small room in the heart of the building. Unusually for me, I was the last one to arrive. My older brothers and sisters were all sitting and chatting at the desks in the front. My little brother cocked his head to one side and looked up at me.

As I listened to my father's lecture, my brush danced across a piece of orange paper, recording the random ideas that naturally popped into my mind. When the lesson was finally over, I started to fold the sheet of paper, but my brother's hand darted in from the side to snatch it from me. I turned around, grinning at his mischievousness, but the look on my little brother's face was serious.

"Sis? What's this?"

"It's nothing. Give it back."

Before I could stop him, he had unfolded the page and sent his eyes racing across the text there. He furrowed his brow.

Ignorant of this little exchange between us, our brothers and sisters left the small room chattering happily. The flames on the candlestands flickered slightly.

"Emigrant? Huh? The ocean? Sis, seriously, what *is* this?"

"Mmm. It's a secret, all right? I mean, I still don't know what's going to happen or anything."

We flew down the passage side by side, toward the old pond in the inner courtyard. We danced down lightly onto its surface. I sat cross-legged on a layer of air just above the cold water, floating. The look on my brother's face as he settled down next to me was uncharacteristically complicated, sunk in thought.

"So, basically, the takezoku are going deeper into the mountains," I said, working hard to keep my voice calm. "But some commoners are building a boat. They're going to go out to sea. Oh! The people you met yesterday. Father actually already knows about all this. He's not going to say anything, though. And so, I, well…"

My brother said nothing.

"So, like…"

"Sis?" He sounded uneasy when he finally opened his mouth to speak.

"They told me that going into the darkness is the same as returning to the past. That they want to go down the river to the land of the future. And it made so much sense to me I wanted to go with them. I mean, we've always lived on this mountain, right? So we don't know any other way to live, you know? And they said going to a new land, living under our own power, would be a real adventure. It'll be hard, but it'll be a fun life. And so, like—" I cut myself off. The wind blew, cold, yanking my long black hair up into the air like a lion's mane. "I asked them to take me with them."

"S-Sis?"

"And then they ended up talking about how they wanted me to come as the monarch of the settler ship."

"So then…this is—" Ever so timidly, my little brother spread out the paper he had nicked from me before, revealing the characters scribbled in black ink.

"Yeah." I nodded slightly.

While we were studying governance with Father, I had been thinking in my own way about rules the takezoku on the settler ship would probably need. Like the sorts of laws we should have if we were going to go to an unknown land and combine our strengths to make a new life. Maybe there should be regular meetings. Also! All of us would be in danger if even just one of us was revealed to be takezoku, so I thought we should have a rule about not leaking our secrets to humans. But what if someone broke one of the rules? Right, there'd have to be serious punishments to match too. And, let's see, there were all kinds of things to think about...

I had moved my pen half in a trance, but suddenly I grew anxious. What if this was just me butting in again? Well, I could simply ask my friends the next time I saw them. We could discuss everything and make the laws we needed.

I drew closer to my brother and gently reached out to touch his soft, pudgy, chilled cheek. "What are you going to do?"

"What?!"

"D-don't act so shocked, all right... If it's easier for you to go into the mountains, then you should do that. But if, if maybe—"

"No way! Crossing the ocean, I totally—Sis, I!" My brother's pale face stiffened as he spoke. He yanked his shoulders back as if trying to escape from me and shook his head from side to side.

"Right!" I hurriedly nodded. "Yeah, sorry."

"I-I-I..."

"What?"

"You—" He hung his head and then yanked it back up. His tone was abruptly hysterical in a way I'd never heard before. "I mean! I don't want you to cross the sea either! I want you to stay with me! I mean, of all our brothers and sisters, you're the only one who really—and then you suddenly say you want to go to the other side of the ocean, I mean, I—! I don't get it."

"Mm."

"I—um. I don't want you to leave me. You dummy." My little brother had no sooner muttered this sad statement than he was turning his back to me and awkwardly racing away down the hall, veering to the left and right. And then he turned into a ball of blue light and disappeared into the darkness, his figure vanishing abruptly, almost with a pop.

Above the pond in the courtyard, still floating, wobbling, cross-legged, I stared at the darkness where he had disappeared and sighed. Tonight again, the moon shone coldly in the night sky, like ice.

◆ ◆ ◆

And then, three days later, the king formally announced the grand plan to transfer the takezoku population deeper into the mountains. The whole community was instantly abuzz, everyone sharing their thoughts on the whole thing with anyone who would listen. But given that the humans and their torches were not going away anytime soon, the people began to accept the need to move away for the sake of peace.

Preparations began all at once in the castle and in the houses outside. Perhaps sensing the change among us, or perhaps for some other reason, the humans began to appear outside the gates in even greater numbers. Some even raised their voices in what sounded like battle cries. The time for the move was closing in on us.

My friends called me to the hut two days after the plan was announced. I woke up when night fell and shot outside. My little brother hadn't spoken to me since I'd told him of the plan, but tonight, maybe feeling a change in the air, he came to me. But when I turned around after landing at the hut, I saw that he had disappeared at some point. I called his name, but my voice was simply swallowed by the darkness. And I was in a hurry, so I gave up on him and went into the hut.

My friends greeted me strangely ceremoniously, which struck me as quite odd.

"What's going on?" I asked.

"Your coronation!"

"...What? Coronation?"

"Well, it's just make-believe, though. Sit, sit!"

The young would-be emigrant takezoku stood crowded together in the hut. In the center was a chair lovingly adorned with seemingly handmade silver ornaments. My friends spoke to me with smiles. "You really came!"

Urged forward, I timidly set myself down on the chair. A large blue handmade hat was placed on my head. It jingled from the decorations that hung from it. Everyone grinned and began to applaud. I was bewildered at first, but my confusion was soon overtaken by delight.

"Everyone!" The girl with the short hair stepped forward on behalf of the group. "Our ship is destined to leave our homeland and be carried away to a far-off country. But destiny has also done something wonderful for us! This princess, whom we all love, the smartest and nicest of the royal family, has deigned to join us on our journey!"

Everyone applauded again. I looked around at their faces, and I gasped with surprise at a sudden realization.

My existence was so worthless, so meaningless, as long as I was among the youngest in the royal family. But now I saw that I was a ray of hope for these future settlers, something that had actual value, a balm on their hearts to relieve the fundamental anxieties and concerns raised by a one-way journey to an unknown land.

The girl raised her voice. "We are about to set out on an incredible voyage! We'll never return alive to these mountains, the eternal homeland of the takezoku. We will be cut off from the long history of our people and become a nation of orphans. But! But! In our hearts—!" Her words were interrupted by the tears spilling out of her eyes.

A man stepped out beside her and held her shoulders as if to give her strength, then picked up where she had left off. "We can live happily anywhere, so long as we have courage in our hearts!"

"And—!" From no one in particular. "Whatever happens, we have a princess with us. We're counting on you for the spring and fall harvest festivals and such."

"But I mean, she's not a princess anymore. She's a queen, right? Well, whatever!"

"Your Majesty the Queen! The ship will be finished soon. So, wait, it's the queen's ship then!"

"This is going to be a fun trip. I mean, it's us. We can be happy anywhere."

"'Cause we're monsters! We're strong! I just know we can make it if we work at it."

Anxiety and hope and faith in each other and the yearning

for an unknown land—all of it mixed together, and the inside of the rough hut began to sparkle.

Made to sit on something like a throne for the first time in my life, I was in a place now where the governance I had studied and the many ideas I had considered would finally be useful. *So will I now have my own country?* I thought with surprise. *Will I have to protect the people and the kingdom?*

Outside the hut, the late winter wind blew fiercely. I heard the clear babbling of the river. Someone poured fresh blood into a vessel, and it circulated through the room.

Gradually, my nervousness subsided. With a gentle smile, I looked around at the bodies—my people, my kingdom. The youth with the book of poetry had come to stand next to me at some point. I looked up at his quiet profile, and he slowly opened his mouth.

"Maybe it was fate."

"Fate?"

"Yeah. You probably think it's a funny beast? But it's like it was all decided in advance, a destiny you share with all of us. So whatever happens next because of it, I'm going to accept it all, good or bad. That's the way I see it."

"You're an idea person, huh?"

"Heh heh. It was written in this book." He showed me the red-covered collection of poetry he was holding so lovingly. And then he met my eyes and grinned playfully.

The coronation turned into a party, the inside of the hut filled with noise and movement, and the night grew ever deeper and darker. The moon radiated a magical blue light. It was indeed a night for monsters.

✦ ✦ ✦

"You fool!"

Before dawn broke, I returned to the castle, went to my father, and reported that I wanted to go out to sea, that I wouldn't be going into the mountains. My brothers and sisters fell silent, so stunned that they appeared to have turned to stone, while my father burned with a fiery rage and roared at me with enough force to very nearly send me flying.

Panicking, I started to fling myself onto my hands and knees before him, as usual, but then checked myself. No. I lifted my face and stared up at my father.

"But I—" My whole body shaking, I tried to express my thoughts. "I...I...I want to go..."

"What are you talking about? You are a royal daughter. And the royal family shall lead the takezoku into the mountains! I will not allow this selfishness!"

"But, Father, you knew about the ship, and you tacitly approved. You didn't punish the commoners."

"You fool, those are peasants. Obviously, this same path is not permitted for you! As a royal, you must go into the mountains, where we shall live a still-quieter life."

"But even if I follow you into the mountains...I-I can never be monarch!"

"What is this nonsense? Aah, I had such hopes for you. You're such a clever child. I see now. You might be very intelligent, but you appear to have no understanding of your place. What poison there is in a daughter's half-finished education..."

"Father?"

"So you want so badly to be king? To intimately wield power? Foolish daughter!"

"I want to be needed!" I shouted, abruptly, from the depths of my heart, the depths of darkness.

My siblings were shocked and floated up from their seats. Perhaps instinctively, they were separating themselves from the anomalous presence that I was, a being to be shunned.

"I want to be needed! I want to be needed! I want to be *needed*! If I can't be of any use to someone, then why have I worked so hard for this knowledge? Why was I born to be a gifted student? Why was I born a girl so unnecessary, so ugly and awkward, unable to pass my days in pleasure like my beautiful sisters? I want to believe that there is a meaning in me being born like this, that it's my destiny. I will rule, I'll be a queen…"

"Queen, queen, queen," my eldest brother said coldly, exasperated. "You mean of those beggars? Come now!"

I looked back at him. I knew that my long black hair flew up and spread out like it was a separate creature with a will of its own. I turned toward my eldest brother, his crossed arms and a sneering expression on his face, and shouted with all my heart, "There are no ranks among the takezoku! And none among the royal family either! We're all supposed to be equal! I-I—I saw that I could be useful to those people about to set out on that journey. If I stay here like this, if I stay here, I-I'll have to act like I'm not here even when I am. I'll have to stay out of your way, keep my head down all the time, hold my breath forever. And that'll be the end for me. Someone, someone…"

Sobs rose up in me, and I said, like spitting blood, "I want to live with purpose! And I know I can. I know it."

"You—!"

"I-I don't want to live like I'm dead anymore. Not one day, not one more day. I'm done."

"Stand up!" my father roared.

I was totally, utterly, completely done. I wouldn't avert my eyes ever again. I forced my head up.

"Such defiant eyes." Father was stunned. "I had misgivings right from the start. That you would be a conceited daughter who would never be brought to heel. That in the end, you would prove to be a fool unable to understand your own place in this world. This impertinent rebellious seed you've kept hidden, I-I've always been aware of it!"

"Father...I-I wanted to be a magnificent ruler like you, Father. From the bottom of my heart, I-I respect—"

"I will not allow it! You are the fifth child of the royal family. You cannot change that destiny." And then, painfully, like he was wringing it out of himself: "Just the way that I must be king like this."

"No!" I stood up and roared back. "A person can change their destiny. I know it, I know it... Because we're alive!"

"Hey?" one of my older sisters interjected, worriedly. "Where do you suppose the boy is?"

"Huh?"

Everyone came back to themselves and looked around. I noticed that my little brother was nowhere to be found. Let's see, when did he leave...? I gasped and stood up. Right, he had followed me part of the way when I was flying along the river at the beginning of the night, but I'd lost sight of him.

Had he seen my coronation? What had happened after that? Ever since I'd talked with him about leaving, he'd seemed too depressed to even talk to me. And yet, lost in the new possibilities for myself, I'd completely forgotten about him.

"He's not in the castle," my sister said, sounding worried. "I thought maybe he went out."

I hurriedly turned my eyes to the sky. Dawn was about to break, wasn't it? I looked around at my father and my siblings. "Um!" I said, pained. "I'll go look for him. He's my responsibility." I bowed once and hurriedly flew out of the room.

The voices of my brothers and sisters chased after me.

"Be careful! It's almost dawn. Wait! I'll come too!"

"Me too. That boy! What on earth could he have gotten up to, I wonder?"

After wrapping myself tightly in my orange light-blocking cloak, I leaped up into a sky on the verge of daybreak. About to go from the castle to the Yellow River, I noticed that the human beings who had been neatly surrounding the castle gates earlier were, for some reason, slipping through them and heading toward the castle. I looked down, incredulous.

"Go back!" I quickly turned around and shouted at my second brother and my sister. "Hurry and tell Father! Look! There! The humans…"

My siblings looked down and gasped. Tentatively, slowly, the humans were proceeding up the gently sloping road to the castle.

One of them noticed us and cried out. Others turned their gazes upward. Shouts of terror and hatred filled the air.

I heard something cut through the air, an arrow passing by my ear. I watched it go, only my eyes not covered by the light-blocking fabric. My sister, flying behind me, twisted her body in surprise to dodge it.

This was followed by rocks being thrown. My second brother caught one of them and casually tossed it back down at the mob. It hit a human in the chest, and he fell to the ground with a thud, vomiting red blood. The humans yelled and shouted, shooting a powerful hatred our way with their glares. Toward the rear was the girl I'd rescued from the fallen tree. She looked up and opened her mouth, *Oh!*

And then bows and guns were turned on us.

I turned neatly aside and flew up into the sky. "Damned humans! They were waiting for morning to attack us! Hurry and tell Father!"

"But what about you?"

"I have to find that boy."

"Got it. So then we'll go back to the castle."

After this back-and-forth, my brother and sister flew off in one direction and I in another, high up in the sky. I passed the castle gates alone and headed toward the river's edge.

People heading for the castle. People scrambling for the common takezoku houses on the riverbank. Of course. The takezoku were without equal at night, but once dawn arrived, we were held back by one tiny weakness. Unable to endure the light of day, we couldn't fight properly once the sun came up.

My friends were in danger too. Soaring above the earth, I raised my voice and announced that we were under attack. The humans who heard me looked up and glared before showering me with arrows and shouting their battle cries at me. Then they brought hunting rifles to their shoulders and peppered me with bullets. Encased in my blackout cloak,

I darted left and right to dodge these attacks. But I had so many near misses. My cloak was riddled with holes in the blink of an eye.

Worried, I cast a glance over my shoulder. From the castle, where the silver towers soared majestically, takezoku wrapped in blackout fabric of various colors shot out and up the mountain. A beautiful sight, a storm of cherry blossom petals. As though their souls were hot despite the fact that they were monsters.

Occasionally, I heard the sound of gunfire. And then takezoku dancing ephemerally like flower petals on the wind fell. Their insides turned to ash, they disappeared in the blink of an eye, and the light-blocking cloak and decorated hat they left behind dropped to the ground.

Grasping the situation from the commotion, peasant take-zoku shot out of the common houses as well. They headed deep into the mountains and instantly receded from sight. From time to time, someone—probably my friends who had chosen the ship over the mountains—would fly toward the opposite bank of the river. Some were hit with arrows, somersaulted in the air, turned to ash, and scattered, while their abandoned cloaks dropped to the ground or the water's surface.

The humans had apparently started to enjoy the hunt, and they ran around shouting as they launched arrows at unresisting takezoku, as they fired their rifles at us.

Turning in midair, I intently sought out my little brother. That kid! Where on earth had he gone at a time like this? I knew he'd followed me at least this far after night fell. He'd looked about to burst into tears. But after that...

When I was almost at my friends' hut on the river, I saw

a scrap of vivid-blue light-blocking fabric behind a tree. I shrieked unconsciously.

He—my brother! He'd already been attacked and turned to dust, vanished. Only a piece of fabric left behind?

But the blue cloth shifted in reaction to my voice. Covering his face very carefully so the sunlight wouldn't touch it, he looked up at me fearfully.

I cried out again in my extreme relief.

My brother seemed relieved too. "Oh! Sis!" he called. A tearful expression on his face, he started to float up.

"No, don't. Stay there. Don't move!"

"Huh?"

"The humans are attacking! You won't be able to get away by yourself. I mean…" *I mean, you…* Unlike me, he wasn't very good at flying. He quickly tumbled and fell from the sky. If the humans found him, he'd be helpless. *Please, just stay there like that.*

I hurled myself toward the ground, a comet burning up and plummeting through the atmosphere. Once I was close enough, I pulled my brother close to me like a treasure. And then I looked up at the sky. I could still see many takezoku flying in the direction of the castle. They ascended along the surface of the mountain and grew distant. No one had known it would be upon us this suddenly, but the end result of the humans' attack was that the time of our move had been moved up to that very morning. Everyone flew with whatever they could carry, without looking back, into the mountains, into the darkness, toward the forest of the past. They fled. In order to survive. They raced away as fast as they could.

My brother and I ran down the alley, shoulders pressed up against each other. The soles of my bare feet hurt. Panting heavily, my little brother gripped my hand tightly. Frightened, he had started to cry.

When we turned the corner heading toward my friends' hut, we came across a group of humans running along from the opposite side. We shrank into the shadows. I looked back at the road we had just come down, but in the blink of an eye, humans had appeared there, too. They saw us and called out happily before readying their guns and bows.

"What? Sis! What is this? Why? We didn't do anything wrong."

"We're about to be killed by ignorance... This way!" I wanted to fly! But if we leaped into the sky now, we'd simply be easy targets for arrows and bullets.

Crouch down and run! Arrows whizzed by on either side of us. My little brother seemed like he would tumble to the ground at any moment. We fled down the alley, finally arriving before my friends' hut. Just beyond it was the boat, a handmade ship to take us away from this country. It was very nearly complete. Aah, but... I put my hand on the door, despaired, cried out. The door was locked from the inside.

"Open up!"

There was no answer. There was no one there.

The humans moved to surround us. I shoved my brother behind me and blocked their path.

"Hey! There's two of 'em over here!" I could heard them shouting to each other. The crowd before us grew larger. The girl was in the front row, and our eyes met again. She shook her head as though uncertain, but then she looked around and readied her weapon, following the lead of her comrades. The humans just kept coming.

At that moment, I remembered, like a revelation. My brother was small enough that he could easily fit through the round hole in the door. Instinctively, I gave up on myself. It was too late.

"Go!" I ordered, in a quiet voice.

"Huh?" my brother asked in reply, extremely perplexed.

"Look, just do what I tell you! Go through the hole into the hut and out through the hole in the back door. And then—right, get on the ship! I'm sure you can do it!"

"Huh? But—"

"We won't be able to make it to the mountains. There are too many humans, and the sun is rising. There's nowhere for us to run now. So hurry up, go!"

"But, Sis!"

"You have to live," I continued, my voice hoarse. "You have to live. The mountains, the darkness, the sea, they will still have a past and a present. As long as you live. As long as you just stay alive for me somewhere. Now hurry! Hurry up and go! Go already!" My roar was tinged with the exact same echo of strength as my father's.

My little brother yanked weakly at my cloak in protest. The humans were inching closer.

I shoved him. Hard. I watched as the vivid blue fabric wrapping his small body slipped safely through the round hole. And then his face popped up on the other side of the hole.

"Hey, c'mon, Sis!" he said, reaching a slender arm out toward me. He looked so worried. My tiny, adorable brother.

"What are you doing?! Hurry up and get on the boat! You have to get on it!"

"No!"

"What? No?"

"Wait!" My brother's face shone as if he'd just hit upon a good idea. "I'll unlock the door. So you can come in—"

"Y-you can't!" I panicked. "If you do, the humans will come in too. Just go. Hurry and get on the boat!"

"No way. I can't just leave you here. I can't!" My brother got serious. His eyes were so clear, so kind. I heard the sound of the lock rattling.

He can't… If I stay here like this, I'll kill my brother…

I turned around. The humans were closing in for the kill. I met the girl's eyes again. Silently, I begged her, *Hurry and shoot! Shoot me!* But even now a light of hesitation flickered across her face, and her arms began to tremble. She simply opened her sad eyes wide, not so much as attempting to shoot. I could hear my brother trying to get the door open. *Aah…*

I closed my eyes.

I braced myself.

I stood blocking the round hole.

"The ship! You have to get on it!" I ordered him one more time. Forcefully, like a king.

But my brother was stubborn like me. "As if I could leave you. No way. I mean, you're my sister. Hold on a sec, I'm almost—"

"Go, my brother!" I prayed from the bottom of my heart. *To the land of the future! Live for me.* That was my sole desire now.

Perhaps realizing what I was about to do, the human girl hurriedly lowered her gun. She opened her mouth wide and reached out to me. I lifted my arms, and the light-blocking

fabric covering my body slowly slid to the ground. I knew
that my entire body was beginning to smoke, to burn in the
light of the sun. And then I vanished.

One last time, with feeling, I called my little brother's
name.

"Ruirui!"

◆ ◆ ◆

I...

I...had a...little brother... A small...one...

*I-I don't want to live like I'm dead anymore. Not one day, not
one more day. I'm done.*

◆ ◆ ◆

*I mean, we've always lived on this mountain, right? So we don't
know any other way to live, you know? And they said going to
a new land, living under our own power, would be a real adventure. It'll be hard, but it'll be a fun life. And so, like—*

I asked them to take me with them.

*And then they ended up talking about how they wanted me
to come as the monarch of the settler ship.*

◆ ◆ ◆

I had a little brother. A small one.

Ruirui.

You will go to the land of the future. And then you will
make your kingdom and stand proudly as king. Don't forget.

A person can change their destiny. I know they can. I just know it.

DAY

There were so many things I wanted to talk to my sister about. I was basically the runt of the royal family—"little Ruirui"—so everyone watched out for me, kept me safe, but I knew well enough that the only one in this world who really loved me in all my misshapenness was my kindhearted sister. My smart, strong sister. The apple of our father's eye, the third princess.

Takezoku live extremely long lives. Which was why I always thought we still had plenty of time to talk. I could just talk with her again tomorrow. Maybe next month. Even next year—or beyond that. Time didn't matter.

But we didn't have any of that left. The moment of our parting came upon us suddenly. Because time just pushes forward, ever forward.

There were so many things I wanted to talk to my sister about. You, my cherished sister. I had things to tell you. So, so many things.

Sis...? Sis!

Sis!

✦ ✦ ✦

"Ruirui!"

With a faint scream, the figure of my sister on the other side of the round hole abruptly disappeared. I had no sooner seen a shower of gray ash erupt than I was watching her cloak sink slowly to the ground, orange and smoldering. Followed by the silver adornments, the proof that she was a noble daughter of the royal family, the hat decorated with long bamboo. It hit the ground with a clumsy jingle.

I heard a human girl scream. I fell on my backside, still gaping. And then a strong wind blew up, bringing in something through the round hole. A folded piece of orange paper settled on my lap.

I picked it up with a trembling hand. Still shaking, I spread it out. Aah, my sister's handwriting.

Memorandum on new laws for the takezoku arrival in the land of the future!

I remembered seeing it that night. Necessary rules and the reasons for them. Proposals for punishments. Although I didn't really understand, I knew when I read it that it was rational and logical, the very thinking of a king, the fruit of the governance lessons we took from our father. And all I had done was burst into tears, afraid that my sister would go far away. I'd been sulking ever since, even though I loved her more than anyone.

I never... That she would go somewhere even further away... The thought had never even entered my mind.

Shaking fiercely, I got to my feet.

People began throwing their bodies against the front door. I heard ferocious roars too. The lock started to give, creaking and groaning in protest.

But I was still just standing there awkwardly. And from the other side of the round hole came the light of death for the takezoku—the pale rays of the morning sun. The light barely touched the tips of my toes, and I felt a searing pain dance across my nerves. But the pain brought me back to myself. Frightened, I inched backward.

And then, and then…

I heard voices from the river behind me. The voices of takezoku calling to their comrades.

I turned around. And then…and then…

Leaving my sister's cloak and finely decorated hat on the other side of the door, clutching just the orange paper tightly to my chest as a memento, I became a beast moving only on the instinct to survive.

I stumbled across the earthen floor. I fell. I groaned. I stood up, and this time, I flew. I had no control; I hit the wall, I tumbled to the ground. I ran again.

Aah, and here the back door was locked too! Tears of dismay sprang up in my eyes. I was a crybaby. All the strength drained out of me, and I slid to the earthen floor. I could no longer move.

I peered through the round hole and saw a large ship on the bank of the river. Takezoku wrapped in light-blocking fabric of all hues were flying in from every direction and racing onto it. The ship was about to set sail. Ah! It was slowly pulling away from the shore and heading out toward the middle of the river…

I started to hiccup. *Sis…* My precious sister had told me to get on the ship. Because I probably couldn't make it safely deeper into the mountains from here. She'd said to live. To live for her.

But. But. Going down the river and out to sea—I couldn't do something that terrifying! I wasn't like my sister. I wasn't like the magnificent third daughter of our king, the talented princess my father was so proud of. I was just the runt…

The ship grew distant, headed downriver. I watched it go in vain.

From outside, the cries of the humans trying to break down the door grew louder. They were flinging themselves against the door. And then it broke and fell to the ground.

The first human was barely inside when I heard him shout, "Whoa! There's one more! The little one in blue!" He immediately nocked an arrow and aimed at me.

I was frozen in place with fear. It was all over. I was ready to close my eyes and give up. It was too late.

And then, I heard the voice of my now-gone sister. *I feel like you being born with that small body, the way you never really grow, I mean, there must be some kind of meaning in that… But when a door closes, a window opens, you know!*

Right. I was the runt. I was smaller than everyone.

I covered myself tightly with my blue cloak and got to my feet. I curled myself into a ball and slipped through the round hole. I flew as hard as I could toward the ship as it slid down the shimmering river. I somersaulted and spun around three times in the air. My head spinning, I couldn't tell which way was what. Just when I thought I'd flown too high, I was plunging into the water. Thoroughly soaked, I managed to drag myself back to the surface and clung desperately to the edge of the ship's hull. Arrows came one after another, followed by bullets. The arrows dug into the side of the ship, and the bullets made their marks with sharp pops.

But my survival instinct was strong.

I gritted my teeth and flew up out of the river. I tumbled onto the deck with a loud thwack. And then a takezoku wrapped in blackout fabric ran out from the stairs leading to the ship's hold to help me and yanked me to my feet. In the next instant, I heard an ominous noise, and several arrows plunged into the place where I had just been.

I heard a shout of "The prince?!" in my ear. Some takezoku held me tightly to cover me. "Hey! The little prince is here! A child of the royal family!" From inside the hold came a sad commotion; it was hard to tell the difference between sobs and cheers.

The ship picked up speed and pulled away from the shore of the river, from the mountains where we had been born and raised, from our homeland, from the past. The humans ran along the bank chasing us, some even going so far as to jump in the water. But the ship appeared to be just a little faster than they were. The settler ship built by the young takezoku slid out of the depths of the mountains, riding the current, and headed down the endless Yellow River.

With the babbling of the river, everything gradually receded. Time. History. Tradition. The pride of the people. The royal family. Our shining memories…

The rough houses of the common takezoku bright in the morning sun. The even rougher human settlement. Desolate wilderness. Another human settlement. Houses of a more modern build here. Expansive forest. A town with large factories. A lovely, seemingly boundless grassland. The scenery flowed by around us. Toward the bright white future.

Up against a wall, I was unable to take even one more step.

I had survived. Just like my sister had ordered me to. I was the only one to survive. All the strength had drained out of my body, and I simply peered out at the flowing scenery.

I remembered what she'd said, my sister now dust and disappeared.

You have to live. You have to live. The mountains, the darkness, the sea, they will still have a past and a present. As long as you live. As long as you just stay alive for me somewhere.

Ruirui!

The glittering surface of the river. The sunlight. Green grasslands spreading out on both sides of the river changed their design each time the wind blew. The colors of the Yellow River were layered, constantly in flux, shimmering and sparkling. Each and every thing I could see was marvelous and beautiful.

I opened my eyes wide, as if seeing a vision of our new life in a distant land. I was no longer afraid of the future.

The survival instinct…

✦ ✦ ✦

Back then, I had a little brother. A small one.

You will go to the land of the future. And then you will make your kingdom and stand proudly as king. Don't forget. A person can change their destiny. I know they can. I just know it.

ABOUT THE AUTHOR

Kazuki Sakuraba was born in 1971. She began publishing while still in college. Her early *Gosick* light novels were best sellers and were translated into English, and her adult fiction is also popular and critically acclaimed. *Red Girls* won the Mystery Writers of Japan Award in 2007 and was translated into English in 2015. *Watashi no otoko*, a suspense novel about an incestuous relationship, won the Naoki Prize for popular fiction in 2008.

Also by Kazuki Sakuraba
and available from Haikasoru:

RED GIRLS

SRP: $15.99 USA / $18.99 CAN / £9.99 UK
ISBN: 978-1-4215-7857-6

When the outlanders abandoned a baby girl on the outskirts of a village, few imagined that she would grow up to marry into the illustrious Akakuchiba family, much less that she would develop clairvoyant abilities and become matriarch of the illustrious ironworking clan. Her daughter shocks the village further by joining a motorcycle gang and becoming a famous manga artist. The outlanders' granddaughter Toko—well, she's nobody at all. A nobody worth entrusting with the secret that her grandmother was a murderer.

This is Toko's story.

www.haikasoru.com